A GOVERNESS' LOT

By Tracy Edingfield

Dedication

This story is for my good friend, Ruth Sheahan, who has already passed, much, much too soon. Her enthusiasm for life, her kind smile, twinkling blue eyes, and silvery-blonde hair made her one of those unique people who are as lovely on the outside as the inside. Ruth's kindness was a treasure and her compassion a gift.

I have missed you, dear friend, and will always miss you. Laugh with the angels, Ruth. I love you.

Acknowledgements

I wish to thank the following people for helping bring the story of Winnie and Charles to life: Lisette Walker, Craig Cillessen, Susanne Lambdin, and Renee Reynolds. Without their patience, I might not have finished this work and I certainly would not have kept my sense of humor. On the days when Winnie and Charles wouldn't speak to me, one of my writing partners would explain why and I'd shuffle back to the drawing board, correct the problem and the lines of communication would re-open. Thanks, dear ones, for being part-interpreter, part-editor and part-sounding board.

For my favorite uncle Spec, who encouraged me when everyone else thought I was nuts to quit practicing law and become a writer, I thank you for the encouragement.

In addition to my friends' contributions, I'm humbled by the love my husband shows me every day—even on the days when I'm not so lovable or haven't had my morning cups of coffee. I couldn't write love stories, Adam, if you hadn't shown me how a real man can love a woman and for that, I simply cannot express my heartfelt gratitude. Thank you for supporting me, making me laugh, and most of all, for loving me.

Tracy Edingfield was born in Wichita, Kansas in 1965 and graduated from the University of Kansas School of Law in 1991. She is a member of Romance Writers of America and the Society of Children's Writers and Book Illustrators and lives in Valley Center, Kansas, with her husband and two sons.

Other Books Written by Tracy Edingfield

The Law Firm of Psycho & Satan

His Sunshine Girl

Prudence

Front Cover Credits

Dane Lowe of Ebook Launch, book cover designer; John and Adrian Lowe of Ebook Launch, formatters; John van Nost, Sculptor; National Trust of United Kingdom, Property Manager of Canons Ashby; Ray Perry, Photographer with this image available at https://flic.kr/p/UVzrGX.

A GOVERNESS' LOT

Chapter 1

Stanhope, County Durham, Northern England
March, 1811

A man's voice bellowed from upstairs. "Blast it! Where are you, Winnie?"

Winsome Montgomery ignored the bellowing of her father's heir, Sir David. She didn't wish to see him and she *really* didn't want him to find her, searching through her father's desk.

He would be livid.

Her instincts warned her that her cousin, Sir David, never pleasant under the best of circumstances, would be wretched if crossed. The man was a bounder.

The voice, closer this time, hollered, "Where could that girl be? Dobson! Where is Miss Montgomery?"

The butler's reply was muffled behind the great oak doors.

Winnie rifled through gaming vowels, unpaid bills, and some letters. Too pressed for time to read the correspondence, she folded the letters then stuffed them inside her bodice.

"There you are, Winnie. Didn't you hear me calling for you?" The new baronet, Sir David, approached. His unrushed footsteps struck the planks, warning of his relentless nature.

A chill skated down Winsome Montgomery's spine. "I should think the whole county heard you, Sir David."

He chuckled, but his eyes remained cold. Her cousin was a tall, handsome man, dressed in the finest apparel offered on Bond

Street. His boots were polished with a champagne blackening mix, an excessive affectation in Stanhope.

"What are you doing in the library, Winnie? I ordered you to remain in your room or the kitchens."

Lowering her eyes, she murmured, "I didn't think you were serious about that."

"You know I was."

Why was the Montgomery name cursed with such scaly baronets? Was the water in the River Wear, which ran through the estate, contaminated with treachery and stupidity?

Tucking a strand of her silver hair behind her ear, Winnie admitted, "I'm searching for my father's time piece. Mama gave it to him and I wished to have something to remember them by."

"This watch?" Pulling a timepiece from his waist coat, he dangled it before her.

"Oh yes! That's it. Thank you very much!"

Snatching it out of her reach, he *tsked*. "It's mine now."

"It's all I have left of my parents," she explained, unable to keep the peevish note from her voice.

"Settle your feathers. Do you want this?"

"Yes."

"Then give me a kiss."

This was worse than she'd dreaded. "What did you say?"

"What's this? No kisses for your cousin?"

It had been a long day. Winnie was in no mood for her cousin's childish games. Folding her arms over her chest, she said, "No. That watch belongs to me. Hand it over."

His expression hardened. He tucked the timepiece back into the pocket of his waistcoat. "Your father gambled everything of value—jewelry, artwork, horses. If I give you the watch, I'll have inherited nothing." He lifted his palms, and inquired in mocking tones, "And then what kind of baronet would I be?"

"A very poor one," she ground out, relishing the double *entendre*. "Those items were sold in contravention of the marriage settlements. They were supposed to be my dowry."

For some mysterious reason, Sir David roared with laughter. Then he shook his head with what could be considered pity—had Winnie believed him capable of such emotion.

9

Pointing to a patch of faded wallpaper above the mantel, he taunted, "Losing the Gainsborough must have been painful, eh, Winnie?"

Winnie choked. "Yes, because my grandmother posed for it. Sir Vernon lost *Landscape in Suffolk* in a game of whist to a soldier."

"Nor a loyal bone in his body, eh, Winnie? Consider, too, all the bastards he sired between here and London."

She managed to not flinch, digging her nails into the palms of her hands.

He whispered, as the serpent did to Eve, "Did you know what one of the guards told me about your father? He said in the weeks Sir Vernon resided in the Fleet that he took wagers, laying odds on the very hour of his death."

She covered her mouth, smothering a cry.

Stepping close, Sir David lifted strands of her hair and played with them. She tried to move away, but he yanked, anchoring her in place.

Tears stung her eyes, her scalp smarting.

The usual coldness left his voice, transmuting into something ponderous as he murmured, "Such an extraordinary color. I've never seen anything like it. As if fairies had stirred melted stars into a pot of liquid sunshine."

The earlier chill returned to Winnie as waves of revulsion swamped her.

Raising the hank of hair to his nose, he inhaled deeply then groaned.

Trembling, Winnie's frightened gaze darted toward the door.

"So sweet," he sighed. "Sometimes when I tup another woman, Winnie, I imagine it's you."

She struggled to break free, but his hold tightened.

His foul breath skidded across her cheek. "I've frightened you, haven't I? No matter. Once you know me better, you'll see that I rather enjoy frightening people."

The baronet captured her hand and forced it onto the hard ridge which formed beneath his pants. He hissed in pleasure. His eyes screwed shut as he pressed her hand up and down the length of his cock.

Horrified, Winnie stiffened her fingers to avoid cupping his manhood.

He pulled her hair. "You'll do as I say or you won't remain at Stanhope."

Bent backward, she hollered for his wife. "Lady Broomstead! Gwyn!"

He laughed without mirth. "My wife, the little mouse, is upstairs. Such a well-dowered, but boring woman. There's something about you that fires my blood, Winnie."

She twisted, but could not break free.

"Become my mistress. I'll provide for you. In exchange, all you have to do is…" Sir David's grip loosened. "Pleasure me."

Wrenching free, she spat out, "My God, you're a swine!"

Whirling away, Winnie hitched her skirts and ran from the library. She sought her room, upstairs. Halfway up the staircase, she felt a vicious pull on her laces. She yelped. Her soles slipped on the riser. Her hands thrust out to regain balance. Spying the landing before her, she knew a sudden dread that she wouldn't reach it. Winnie's hands clawed through air. Another strong yank on her laces and she lost her foothold. Tumbling backward, she cracked her head on a step. Cartwheeling and screaming, she spied the ceiling then the wall, jolting each time she struck the hard steps. Sir David shouted a string of curses. Blindly, she reached for a stairway spindle, but it sailed past. She flung her arm behind her to stop her momentum, landing on it when she came to rest. A sickening 'pop' and she screamed in agony.

Winnie's heartbeat thudded through her veins. Her screams dwindled to whimpers as she rocked on the floor, cradling her arm.

The commotion summoned the butler, Dobson, at a dead run. "What's happened?"

Sir David prodded Winnie with the toe of his boot as if she were some oddity displayed at the county fair. "Winnie must leave Stanhope immediately and forever. She's a damned bore. Dobson, take her to town in the cart, but know this: I won't pay the doctor's bill for the clumsy cow."

11

"Is she to have any purse, Sir David?"

"No. Let the bitch contrive on her own." The baronet spun away and slammed the library door behind him.

Bile rose and Winnie bit her lip to keep it down. She'd known not to trust her cousin, but she hadn't expected him to be this...this evil.

Dobson touched the top of Winnie's head, silently asking if she was all right.

She stared at the man she'd long considered family. "He...he threatened to make me his—" Here she shuddered. "Mistress."

"And when you refused, he threw you down the stairwell." Dobson's lower lip curled in contempt. He didn't ask, but rather he stated it, showing a plain understanding of her cousin's dastardly nature.

"Pulled me, more like."

"There are no words for men of his ilk," the butler muttered. "At least, none I can repeat in your presence."

The rueful way he said it made her smile.

"Do you realize, Dobs, you're the only man I've known to be loyal and kind? You remain, even though Sir Vernon hasn't paid your wages in months."

He scooped her up, and carried her to the kitchen.

With sorrow in her voice, she said, "My father wasn't an honest man. If he wasn't lying outright, then he prevaricated. He didn't respect the truth any more than his wedding vows and his heir is proving to be worse."

"Aye, a pair of scoundrels."

Her father had been a lying, gambling womanizer who made his wife miserable. Her cousin would be just the same. Meanwhile, this butler was worth ten of such baronets.

Mrs. Dobson, the butler's wife and cook of Stanhope, scurried into the room. "What's wrong?"

"Sir David attacked Winnie when she refused to be his mistress."

The woman's eyes widened to saucer-size. "He did WHAT?" Glancing about the room, she spotted the rolling pin.

She latched onto it and headed toward the door with it raised in militant fashion.

"Here now. Time enough for that later." He disarmed his wife then consoled her. "You can poison his soup at dinnertime, I promise."

Disgruntled, but resigned, she mumbled, "Promise?"

Shaking his head in mock reproof, he said, "Tend to Winnie's arm, my love."

"It's broken," Winnie volunteered, heartened by their stalwart defense. "I heard it pop."

"Good heavens!"

Setting down the rolling pin, Dobs muttered he'd go hitch the pony cart.

The housekeeper clucked about Winnie then announced she must fetch some linens. When she returned, Winnie noted it was with a brand new set of sheets. They belonged to Sir David.

"Stripped them right off his bed, I did."

Winnie smiled. Her father's gambling had decimated the household budget so that new linens were beyond their means. The sheets of Stanhope had been mended several times over. Let Sir David sleep on those a few nights.

"Perfect."

Mrs. Dobson wrapped her arm as tightly as she could, then cradled it in a sling. Once that was accomplished, the housekeeper swore beneath her breath as she packed Winnie's things. Luggage was another luxury they couldn't afford at Stanhope, so the cook filled a basket with Winnie's belongings. Her husband returned to load it. Dobson assisted his wife into the bed of the cart. She laid out a blanket—also stolen from the baronet—then signaled for Winnie. Slowly, she made her way to the wagon. With Dobs' assistance, Winnie climbed aboard and rested her head into Mrs. Dobson's lap, grateful for the cushioning.

Dobs heaved himself onto the bench, clicked his tongue against his teeth, and set the cart into motion.

Her arm hurt like the devil, but the physical pain blotted out the emotional havoc of being expelled from her childhood home. Raising her head, she stared at Stanhope. White, slow-moving dots along the pastures reminded her the sheep needed to be sheared once the weather turned. The river curved through granite, carving out a crevice wide enough to take away the melting snows of winter. She closed her eyes to better hear the gurgling water and bird song. She wouldn't be here for another shearing or again walk across the stepping stones in the narrow portion of river.

The pony cart rocked side-to-side, carrying her away from all she held dear.

Her whole world centered upon Stanhope and the Montgomery estate. While her father gamed in London, she lived alone, not having a London Season or even attending local assemblies. Her father, Sir Vernon, hectored about the outrageous expense. He never mentioned she had a dowry nor revealed he'd used it to fund his entertainments. She'd only learned that upon his death when the solicitor revealed it.

No wonder Sir David laughed when she mentioned her dowry. It had never been Sir Vernon's intention to see her married; he'd done everything possible to ensure she'd remain a spinster.

"Where will she go?" Mrs. Dobson asked.

"She can stay for a few days with Dr. Kessler, I'm sure." Her husband rubbed his chin. "After that? London. Go to London, Winnie, and find a position."

"Edward! She's got no money to travel to London and why should she? Winnie should find herself a husband, settle down."

"There's no one around here that I *could* marry. Even Squire James would expect a dowry." Winnie closed her eyes, trying to blot out the picture of their neighbor's enormous belly and bald head. If that were the only male she could marry, she'd rather stay single. "Not that I wish to place myself at the mercy of another man."

"But a woman alone—"

"And a pretty one, to boot," Dobs interjected.

Winnie retrieved the wad of papers and handed then to Mrs. Dobson. "I was searching for Sir Vernon's watch and found these. Maybe one of my father's correspondents will help me find a position."

"Oh, my stars!" Mrs. Dobson shrieked. "Winnie! Winnie!"

"Owww!" Winnie cried, doubled over in agony.

"Oh." Mrs. Dobson covered her mouth, instantly contrite. "I'm sorry. I wasn't thinking."

"Quit smacking the girl and tell me what's got you so excited," growled Dobs, twisting around to glare at his wife.

With the air of a victorious warrior, Mrs. Dobson raised her fist, which clutched a letter. "There's twenty-five pounds in here!"

"Have you been nipping the brandy, Gloria?" Dobs brought the cart to a halt.

"Yes!" She beamed at Winnie then cast an annoyed look at her husband. Reading from the letter, Mrs. Dobson said, "Sir Vernon, I thank you for sending the painting. My wife adores it already. It takes pride of place in our drawing room. However, I feel the value of the painting exceeds the amount of our particular debt, so I enclose this sum in the hopes that my conscience will be clear. Good luck in your future endeavors. Signed…" She squinted, bringing the paper closer to her face. After a few seconds of fruitless deciphering, she showed it to Winnie. "Can you make out that signature?"

Winnie's forehead puckered. "Good heavens! Is that a 'G' or a 'D?' Maybe an 'O?'"

"Look, Edward. What's that squiggle say there?" Mrs. Dobson handed over the letter.

Dobs glared at the plain sheet of paper then announced, "I've seen chickens scrawl neater than this."

Mrs. Dobson snorted, snatching the letter back. "Well, who cares who the fellow is? You've got twenty-five pounds, Winnie. No need to worry how you'll get to London now, dearie. Why, just imagine. You'll be able to purchase a dress—even a woolen cloak!"

"Thank God for the kindness of a stranger," Winnie murmured.

Pointing at her, Dobs said, "Find yourself a teaching position at a seminary or finishing school. You'll be safe amongst the other ladies, not where any blighter can lay his hands on you." Dobs faced forward, flicking the reins to give the old horse the signal to continue the journey to town.

"That's an excellent suggestion, Dobs. You both will need to find new positions, too. I shouldn't think my cousin will keep you on."

"I wouldn't work for him, even so." Mrs. Dobson said, glaring at her husband's back.

He must have sensed the scorch between his shoulder blades for without turning around, he drawled, "Quite true. Now that Mrs. Dobson has revealed homicidal tendencies, I could never trust her with that rolling pin so long as Sir David is present."

Despite her pain, Winnie had to smile.

Perhaps if she were surrounded by a classroom of tykes, she need never feel alone again. Cheered by the prospect, she watched the gates of Stanhope disappear from view then sagged against Mrs. Dobson. As the wheels turned and the river rushed alongside them, she fancied the cart wasn't so much carrying her away, as moving her forward.

Chapter 2

A roadside inn near Sheffield, England

Sitting in the dimly-lit parlor, Winnie nibbled on an almond biscuit kindly provided by the innkeeper. As she lingered over her cup of tea, she made no effort to hide the fact that she listened to another's private conversations. At first, she had tried to ignore them, but the men's voices carried through the paper-thin walls from the adjoining room.

An army captain and his batman bickered as they played cards for outrageous sums. From what she understood, this was not an infrequent past time for the pair.

"Captain! You can't be serious—you bet a hundred on that hand?"

A hundred pounds? That was several years' salary for most people! Winnie *tsked*.

"I deserve to be shot," said the captain, speaking in a lower register than his batman.

Winnie agreed. Had her father lived, this captain fellow might well have been his jail mate in the Fleet. Oh, joy.

"Shall we play again?"

"Certainly, Spec. Only raise the stakes to ten. I feel lucky."

Harrumphing at such foolishness, Winnie then polished off her tea and biscuit. She looked for the innkeeper, wondering if he would refresh the pot. By now the tea was stone-cold. She gazed at her companion, Mrs. Sheridan, the wife of a vicar. Her tea remained untouched while she snored.

Pity, that.

"Pour us another whisky." Again, she identified the captain. He was used to issuing orders. An unattractive quality, as if being a gambler weren't bad enough, but he did have a lovely, rich timber to his voice.

She closed her eyes, trying not to focus on the dull ache in her arm. If only she could become comfortable. Rather than dosing herself with laudanum, she'd chosen to remain alert on her travels so she could safeguard her belongings. Meager as they were, that basket contained everything she owned. Now with the coach requiring repairs, held up in the private sitting room of this not-too-fastidious inn, Winnie regretted not taking her pain medicine.

"Mr. Bannock?" She rose, approaching the door, but her voice wasn't overly loud. It didn't seem polite to holler for the innkeeper. She would ask for more tea when he appeared, as surely he would soon. She'd also ask how much longer they'd be expected to wait for the wheelwright.

Sighing, she returned to the small chair, pulling it closer to the fire. The warmth was soothing. She'd like nothing better than to slip between cool sheets, nestle against a pillow and sleep for a week. Ascertaining that Mrs. Sheridan slept on, Winnie massaged her stiff shoulder. She delved through her reticule and withdrew her laudanum. Carefully, she pulled the cork from the bottle and took a quick sip. Usually, opium syrup is mixed with a glass of water. Now she knew why. The taste was horrid! Bitter bile filled the cavern of her mouth and she frantically looked about for something to wash the awful stuff down her throat.

Her gaze lit upon Mrs. Sheridan's cooled tea. She rushed, as quietly as she could, to the small, inlaid table and picked up the cup, swallowing the contents all at once.

Then she sputtered, gasped. A trail of fire burned her gullet. Whisky!

What a ripe gudgeon she was not to notice the vicar's wife was a secret tippler. Her ability to sleep anywhere, at any time, was no longer to be wondered at, she thought in disgust.

Gulping several times, the whisky burned away the bitter taste of laudanum like swallowing a fireball.

Another burst of laughter. The chinking of coins passing hands. The thudding of a bottle being set down hard on the table.

Yes, those fellows next door were having a grand time. The voices, indistinct now, rumbled. Her ear trained on each one: Spec, the batman, who spoke with the slightest accent—from where, she didn't know; Nancy, the serving girl, whose speech was interlaced with annoying giggles; two other men whose identity remained unknown; and the captain whose low voice pleased Winnie's ear. She imagined what a delight it would be to hear the man read poetry aloud.

"Whisky, Spec! Nancy, give me a kiss. There's a good girl."

Winnie sniffed then began pacing. She deplored gamblers and wasn't overly fond of drunks and rakes. The captain embodied all those useless qualities. To herself, she could admit she enjoyed listening to the man's voice, but she was rather glad she didn't have to meet him face-to-face. Stuck in the backwoods awaiting a carriage, she might be at loose ends, but didn't wish to meet a man cut from the same cloth as her father, Sir Vernon, and her cousin, Sir David.

The talk ceased as the party, no doubt, consulted their cards. Winnie couldn't see the occupants next door, but having listened to them this past hour, she had a fairly good idea of their activities. The captain was working his way through the bottle while he flirted with the barmaid. Spec, his batman, raked in the coins, and also twitted Nancy. She frowned, recalling she'd heard both men make up to the woman.

Winnie caught a glimpse of the serving girl after the innkeeper brought in the tea tray, an hour before. Nancy's blouse had big, puffy sleeves. One sleeve drooped off the shoulder and she constantly tugged the front of her blouse, which strained across her bosom. The combination of tightness and bare shoulder seemed to be an advertisement of sorts. As Winnie wondered about Nancy's ill-fitting clothes, Mrs. Sheridan muttered something. Although Winnie had never heard the phrase 'light skirt,' she sensed it was negative reflection upon the girl's character.

"But captain! We've just arrived in Sheffield!"

"Don't you want to return to London?" The captain's deeper voice asked.

"I know what all this is about—you're wishing to get back to those bits of muslin! Who'd you fancy? The opera dancer? The blonde one with legs?"

"They all have legs, Spec. Otherwise, I should imagine they'd be poorly suited as opera dancers."

Winnie bobbed her head from side to side. It was an egregious thing to say, but the captain had a point.

Mrs. Sheridan's nostrils quivered, the folds in her throat causing her escaping breath to vibrate in a most unpleasant manner. Winnie inspected the creases in the lady's voluminous skirts. It's possible she concealed a small silver flask in the pocket of that garment, using her ample figure to avoid detection.

Winnie massaged her arm, contemplating how long it would take before the laudanum's effect took hold. With the coach's constant jostling, it ached prodigiously.

She heard the captain say, "Don't listen to this fool, Nance. You know London ladies don't tempt me."

"Oh, Charles, I didn't fall off the turnip wagon."

The captain chuckled.

A feminine squeal followed, as if the barmaid had been pinched or grabbed around the waist. Winnie couldn't be sure, but a flush rose in her cheeks. It was all very improper, whatever was going on in the gaming room.

From the doorway, she glanced about the parlor, her disinterested gaze lighting again on the vicar's snoring wife, Mrs. Sheridan, who occupied most of the sofa. Same as in the coach— Mrs. Sheridan hogged the bench seat, to Winnie's chagrin.

Again, she wondered how long they would be delayed. It would appear an overnight stay would be required in this dreary inn. If she were to guess, Nancy, the barmaid, was also responsible for ensuring the guests' comfort. From what she had witnessed of Mr. Bannock's establishment, Winnie held no confidence that his standards of hospitality would match hers.

She gave a heartfelt sigh, weary to her bones.

In the corridor, the maid, Nancy, was backing out of the room, wiggling her fingers 'goodbye' at the gaming fellows. They tried to detain her, calling out, "Don't leave now, Nancy!" or "It's just getting interesting."

Winnie pursed her lips. She certainly wasn't going to stand by and allow the gamesters to monopolize the only servant she'd seen for the past hour. She stepped up and tapped Nancy's bare shoulder. "Excuse me, miss—"

The serving girl whirled about to face her. Nancy's eyes widened and she tried to block the view inside, but Winnie peeked, curiosity being one of her besetting sins. Smoke clouded the air. Several whisky-hazed men slumped about the gaming table.

Nancy snapped the door shut then re-tucked her blouse into the waist band of her skirt.

Apparently, there was more 'activity' going on in that room than Winnie had imagined.

"If you please." Winnie's voice became sharper, a result of embarrassment. And—if she were honest—her grumpiness was owing to needing restorative sleep. Her arm truly ached.

The brunette's head lifted, eyes narrowing upon her.

So much for friendly service from the barmaid.

"If you please, would you locate the coachman and ask if the axle's been fixed?"

"What do you mean?"

Taking a breath and reminding herself patience was a godly virtue, Winnie explained, "I mean, we've been here—Mrs. Sheridan and I—for the past hour." She waved her hand to indicate her companion's presence. "If the axle hasn't already been repaired, I suggest—much as I dislike the notion—that you show us to a room where we can retire. We'll resume our travels in the morning."

There. Surely the ninny would understand now. Winnie's hope died when the bovine expression remained on Nancy's face.

"Repair the axle? Sheffield has no wheelwright." The barmaid spoke in a breathy tone which made Winnie want to shake the girl.

"No wheelwright? What arrangements has the coachman made to have the axle repaired?"

Nancy shook her head.

Winsome tried again. "Has he caused a message to be sent to the nearest wheelwright? No? Well, is there anyone available who could make the repairs? Will another coach travel by tomorrow, which could take us up?"

The barmaid's blank look began to wear on Winnie's nerves.

Unable to put both of her fists on her hips, Winnie settled for the one and doubled up glaring at the chit. "Let me guess. You don't know. Well, Nancy, will you show Mrs. Sheridan and me to a room?"

The door to the gaming room opened.

Winnie turned her head, noted the broad frame of a dark-haired gentleman standing in the doorway then resumed glowering at the serving wench. It was only upon her second, involuntary glance that she realized how much the man's striking figure filled the space. His broad shoulders were fully displayed as he'd already shed his jacket. His linen shirt, made with a very fine weave, gaped at the throat. Highly improper—he must have discarded his neck cloth during his game of cards. His right hand appeared to have been mauled. Long, muscular legs drifted from a tapered, trim waist to end in a pair of highly-fashionable, highly-polished Hessian boots.

Her gaze lifted to his face. His hair was mahogany brown, long enough that its ends curled. The eyes, also brown, twinkled at her. The mouth with a full, sensuous bottom lip curled in an appealing grin.

"Well, well. What do we have here?" The man's eyes gleamed as his gaze roamed Winnie's form.

Fret lines appeared in the grooves flanking Nancy's mouth. She wasn't a particularly bright girl, but she cottoned on quickly she had a rival for the captain's admiration.

Winnie shook her head, scattering foolish notions of listening to this man read poetry. There was nothing remotely domestic about the blighter. To be certain, he was handsome, but Winnie could have gotten drunk on his whisky-fumed breath. She checked herself in mid-thought: was it possible she was smelling her own breath? Blast Mrs. Sheridan!

"I…" Her voice sounded like the ear-splitting noise a cat makes after having its paw trod on. She gave a tight smile then began again. "I am a passenger in the mail coach. Mrs. Sheridan and I." She pointed inside the parlor to indicate the slumbering matron. "It's late and we wish to retire for the evening, if the axle can't be mended soon. Do you know whether the axle has been repaired?"

Again, that charming smile flashed at Winnie.

"Charles?" Nancy snugly placed her body against his side.

He winked at the serving girl, silently assuring her not to worry about two paltry female customers.

The daughter of a baronet bristled at his dismissive attitude.

"I expect you'll need to hire the room, Miss?" He cocked an eyebrow, waiting for her to provide her name.

Winnie ignored his silent request.

"If you will kindly *listen to me*, I have asked whether you know if the repairs are completed. Do you?"

"Do I what?"

Winnie's patience snapped. "Where is the coachman?"

He jerked his dark head toward the room, motioning her to enter.

She leaned forward, sidestepping the limpet on his arm. "Good heavens!"

On the floor sprawled the coachman, face-down. Another man, presumably the batman, draped over a chair while Mr. Bannock, the innkeeper, slept with his head resting on the table.

"Nance, put Miss…Miss…"

Whether he forgot what he was going to say or whether he was shocked into silence by her angry stare, Winnie couldn't tell and didn't care.

Very much on his dignity, he shot the cuffs on his linen shirt then asked, "Beg your pardon, ma'am, what did you say your name was again?"

Glaring at him, Winnie didn't hide her disdain.

He shifted his weight on his feet and tucked his damaged hand behind his back, the very picture of guilt.

She rolled her eyes. That he should be vain about what was so obviously a war wound was beyond ridiculous. He should be ashamed, rather, for getting drunk and pawing the help.

"You enticed my coachman to play cards and get drunk with you," she summarized the captain's evening.

"No, I didn't." His lips firmed in annoyance. "Look, Miss Whoever You Are—"

Her gaze slid past him, cutting short his stream of foolishness.

"A room, please?"

Rather than comply with the patroness' request, the ninny hammer Nancy looked toward Captain Charles for guidance. That kind of brainless female always looks to a man to solve her problems, Winnie noted in disgust.

"Put the two crones in one of the rooms," he said to Nancy, giving her waist a squeeze. "Then meet me in the other one."

Winnie gasped. "That was uncalled for!"

The captain made a bow, as if in apology. That intention crumpled with his next words. "That was remiss of me. Nancy, put Mrs. Sheridan and the crone in a room together."

Nancy's giggle lit the fuse on Winnie's temper.

"You're insufferable!" she snapped.

"Captain!" A man wailed from the card table then cast up his accounts.

Captain Charles Whatever His Name Was backed away, turning craven once his man shot the cat.

Winnie grabbed the captain by the shirt tail and stayed his departure. "Oh, no, you don't!"

"He's sick," he protested.

"Yes, I know that, you idiot! Anyone would know that! But you must be the one to lift him and get him out of here."

Faint choking sounds escaped the sick man.

Nancy giggled.

The captain glared at Winnie. "Spec's done this countless times before. I know how to handle this." He stepped over the moaning man, grabbed him by the back of his waistband and hauled him a few feet from his puddle of sick. Brushing his palms, as if he'd performed a labor-intensive chore, he declared, "There. Now, Nancy, what say you and I—"

"You can't leave him like that!"

24

His eyes narrowed to angry slits.

Winnie stomped her foot. "Is this man in your employ?"

Wary of responding to what could be a trick question, he admitted, "Yes."

"And has he been a faithful servant to you, Captain?"

Again, he seemed reluctant to answer. Grudgingly, he agreed.

Nodding as though she knew his answer all along, Winnie then spun on Nancy and ordered her to clean up the mess. "It's your job, isn't it?"

"But…but…"

"Your job?" Winnie stressed the second word. "For heaven's sake, don't just stand there. Go fetch a pail of water and scrub brush. Bring the poor man an ale and handkerchief."

Nancy covered her shoulder, tugging her sleeve before flouncing off, presumably to do Winnie's bidding.

Growling, the captain picked up his cohort and led him to a chair, into which he half-thrust and partly allowed him to collapse. He lifted Spec's chin and tilted his head all the way back. The captain stepped back to view that pose. Not satisfied, he shook his head then carefully brought Spec's shoulders forward until his forehead, like the innkeeper's, rested on the table. He congratulated himself. "Right as rain!"

"Not right as rain," Winnie said between her teeth. "You are either the stupidest man I've ever met—and let me assure you that's no easy achievement—or the most disloyal."

His head swiveled toward her and his eyes flashed with anger. Suffering a belated reaction to the sharp movement, he winced. Both of hands clamped over his ears as if to prevent his head from wobbling off his neck. "Damn you."

He made as if to step around his companion, but his boots slid in the puddle of sick and he swore a long, blue streak. Too late, the captain recalled her presence and mumbled, "New boots, don't you know?"

"Serves you right." Winnie returned to the parlor, slamming the door so loudly Mrs. Sheridan roused from slumber.

"What? What?" The tippler's head whipped around as she tried to orient herself.

"We are stuck here for this evening," Winnie ground out. "We have been left to our own devices and must find a room to share."

"Oh."

Mrs. Sheridan blinked a few times then galvanized into action. "Well, shall we retire then? I've had a lovely snooze, but confess, I long for bed. Poor Matthew, he'll be so disappointed I've been delayed."

Winnie resolved to be kinder to the older woman. She was as exhausted as Winnie and it wouldn't do to get crossways with her. Mrs. Sheridan would be with her on the remaining journey to London, another two days. So, Winnie summoned the strength from somewhere and smiled at the vicar's pickled wife.

"Do you have a valise? You might have to carry it upstairs. The innkeeper and his meager staff are…indisposed."

"Oh, certainly, I can." She rose, but before she could put word into deed, the captain appeared on the parlor's threshold wearing his coat. If he'd desired to score points for improving his appearance, he was sadly mistaken. With his neck cloth still absent, Winnie didn't look upon him favorably.

Seeing her glittering gaze, his voice came out in a coat of ice. "Excuse me, miss, ma'am."

"Yes?" Mrs. Sheridan asked.

"May I assist you with your luggage?"

Winnie harrumphed. She preferred him better as a drunken idiot than a toadeater. This display of patent insincerity did him no credit.

He walked into the room, and by lifting his brow, inquired if he could carry Mrs. Sheridan's valise.

"Thank you," she told him then urged Winnie, "Let him carry your things, dear."

"No, thank you. I'll do it myself." Winnie snatched her basket from his grasp and, with her good hand, pressed it against her stomach.

"Don't be daft," he snapped.

Captain Charles lifted the basket onto his shoulder, tucked Mrs. Sheridan's valise beneath his arm, and led them upstairs.

Hovering on the threshold of what appeared to be the best room in the establishment, Winnie sniffed the stale air in the room then stalked to the bed and flung the covers back, running her hand along the linen.

"Are the sheets damp, dear?" Mrs. Sheridan asked.

"No. Although the room could use an airing."

The captain rolled his eyes then left.

Belatedly, Winnie remembered to thank him, but he was already gone. Returning to the card game or Nancy. He clearly intended to tup her that evening.

Mrs. Sheridan cracked the window to allow fresh air into the room and within a short time, the ladies had changed into their nightgowns.

Winnie longed to have a cup of tea before retiring. Even a glass of ale would be welcomed if it washed the taste from her mouth. In the morning, before taking her leave of Mr. Bannock, she would be sure to let him know just what she thought of his inn's poor service. She's also give the coachman a solid tongue-lashing, as well. Without anything more to do, though, she climbed into bed, planning how best to deliver these set-downs.

Mrs. Sheridan fell asleep, showing she had a real gift for the art of slumbering. Resentfully, Winnie glowered at her bed mate then regretted turning her head for the laudanum made the room spin.

She closed her eyes, and began counting sheep. At least a dozen woolly creatures had leapt over a hedge before Winnie sat bolt upright and cupped her hand to her ear.

"Damn her!"

The echo of the captain's curse, his pounding footsteps, and a horse's neigh made her lips curl upward.

Soon after she heard a loud 'thump,' a groaned curse then the captain swearing at his batman. 'Stay on the damned horse, Spec!'

Winnie was sent to slumber with a grin on her face as two horses trotted from Mr. Bannock's establishment.

Chapter 3

Kedington, England

"Oh, Lord, Spec, what have I done?" Captain Charles Dryden nearly sat up before collapsing onto his pillows. He clamped the sides of his head in a futile effort to keep it from throbbing. Slitting his eyes open, he watched his valet place his shaving implements at right angles. Spec might appear uncouth, but he was straight as a die, through and through. And one of the most hard-headed drinking men he'd met. Spec must have already taken his obnoxious, brewed remedy; that would account for his ability to function while standing upright.

By slow degrees, Charles moved his head to avoid sloshing his still-foxed brain.

"Be specific, if you don't mind, captain."

Charles Dryden, a war hero and younger brother to an earl, smacked his lips together. "There's an odd taste in my mouth," he complained.

Spec rubbed his chin.

Charles didn't trust the mischievous gleam in his valet's eye. "That could have something to do with the whisky we consumed last night..."

He nodded then his eyes widened in horror before Spec finished his teasing.

"Or you could be tasting the earful that young lady shoved down your throat."

"You mixed your metaphors."

That silvery-headed miss—the one who'd refused to give her name—how she despised him. Groaning, he prayed, "God help me."

"I don't think He'll bother," said his valet, whistling as he gathered the captain's boots. He stopped whistling a cheery tune, wrinkled his nose then whistled again—a long, piercing noise which shattered Charles' eardrums.

"Oh, God," Charles moaned again.

"You keep calling His name, but I doubt He's in the mood to listen. Like as not, He's as disgusted with you as that lady." Spec grinned. "Why, I've never seen the likes! *Tsk, tsk.* Imagine! You hiked how many miles along the Iberian Peninsula in your old boots, return to England to have a pair made by Hoby and they don't last a league."

Swinging his legs over the edge of his bed, Charles snapped, "You can stop *tsking*! I swear you're just as annoying at the chit!"

"The pretty one?"

"Yes, dammit."

But Spec was not to be subdued, to his employer's chagrin. He prattled on, relishing the chance to paint the blank canvas which was Charles' memory. "The pretty, silver-haired lady who thinks you're stupid?"

"Yes, her. Blast you."

"The one you insulted by calling a crone then swore at? That one?"

"I did? Oh God, I did." Charles mumbled, too foxed to even hang his head in shame.

Narrowing his eyes, Spec exhibited a schoolmaster's ruthlessness in scolding when he reminded Charles, "You remember she had a broken arm? That she was the only one at Bannock's who had a care for me?"

"That's not true! I did—"

"You dragged me from my crumpets only because she harangued you to do so, Captain, and you know it."

"Should I have read a fairy tale then put you to bed? Dammit, Spec, I brought you home, didn't I?"

"After you let me fall off my horse."

29

Charles rubbed the back of his neck. "That was an accident."

His valet sniffed, showing he wasn't ready to forgive him yet. "I don't often shoot the cat and you know that for true."

"I know. I know. It's just…I was pretty randy last night…"

"That was clear to everybody, I should think." The fellow whistled. "But Fancy Nancy? Like as not, you'd piss fire for months after tupping her."

Charles had no intention of showing his agreement with that assessment. He didn't know what had gotten into him last night. It must have been the whisky…or the prognosis that enhanced the barmaid's charms.

He rose from the bed slowly, the noon sun shining through the window. He tested his legs to see if they could take his weight. Relieved to find they could, Charles said, "Let's put off the trip to London, eh? It's too late to leave today, anyway. And bring me your concoction. My head aches like the devil." He pulled on his dressing robe, tying the belt in a clumsy knot.

"Already done." Spec handed him a glass of the murky brew.

He stared down, not knowing what ingredients Spec used in the concoction, nor wishing to discover them. After years of being with his batman, Charles wouldn't have been surprised if Spec ground up Eye of Newt or something of the like. Steeling himself, he guzzled the contents.

Peeling back the layers of hazy fog, he recalled the silvery-blonde who'd taken him in such dislike, which was a shame.

"She was a pretty parcel, wasn't she?"

"Who?"

"The icicle at Bannock's."

"Aye, Captain, but she's no liking for you. 'You're either the stupidest man I've ever met—and let me assure you that's no easy achievement—or the most disloyal.'" Spec mimicked. "Not that you can blame her. Why were you so rude to her? Not yourself, if you ask me."

His brows gathered as he marshalled his feeble thoughts to consider the question. He had been intolerably rude to the miss last

30

evening. Aha! He'd referred to her as miss, seeking her name three times. Every time she had cast him such a look of loathing, it needled. She'd actually rolled her eyes when she saw his wounded hand. That stung more than he cared to admit, so he'd called her a crone. Twice.

Oh Lord! His mama would blister his backside for this.

Charles nodded, acknowledging the truth of his valet's statement. He had become bad-tempered since seeing his brother's physician. The good doctor informed him he'd no longer be able to return to combat. Soldiering had suited him well until recently. Watching men fall in battle had so inured him to loss he wondered if he were capable of feeling anything. Nightmares of Busaco haunted him, assuring him he still possessed a soul, albeit a tortured one. Charles was at a loss to imagine his future if soldiering weren't a part of it. It was all he'd known.

There was a knock at his door at the same time it flung open. "Good morning, darling brother!"

One hand went to Charles' temple while the other motioned his brother to be quiet. "Please, Will!"

The Earl of Northampton, though, rubbed his palms together briskly and asked in a much too hearty voice, "What's this? Am I disturbing your peace? Funny how that didn't concern you sots at one o'clock this morning. By the by, whatever made either one of you think you could sing?"

Alarmed, for Charles recalled nothing of that—he cast a quick glance at Spec, who was rapidly shaking his head, denouncing it. "Impossible!"

Relieved to hear this denial, Charles scowled at his brother and repeated, "Impossible."

Humming a few bars, Will traipsed into the room then began singing off-key. *Forgive me if I praise those charms, thy glaziers bright, lip, neck, and arms…*

Clasping the earl's shoulder, Spec sang, *The snowy bubble e'er appear…*

*Like two small hills of sand…*Charles' boomed.

Altogether, they finished in close harmony. *My dear*

They broke apart, sharing a laugh.

Spec fetched his clothes for the day while Will took a seat by the small table. The earl lifted the silver pot, asking Spec, "Coffee?"

"No, but thank you, my lord," the batman replied, tossing Charles' breeches onto the bed.

Charles' lips twitched as the earl lifted his brows at the blithe response. He invited his brother, "By all means, help yourself to a cup."

"With your permission," the earl said in a dry voice.

Absent-mindedly, Charles rubbed the back of his hand, which ached. He must have strained it hauling Spec onto his horse.

His brother, upon seeing this, asked, "Does your hand pain you?"

Charles turned his hand over, palm side down. His pinky had been sliced off, along with a chunk from the back so that it looked like a big-jawed animal had taken a bite of him.

"It's stiff as hell and aches whenever it rains."

"Which is daily during an English spring."

"True," Charles owned.

"What did the doctor say?"

His smile became forced. The news from the doctor was the primary reason he'd chosen to over-imbibe the night before.

"After several annoying tests, he addressed me as the Honorable Charles Dryden. Does that answer your question?"

Will grimaced in sympathy. "So that means you'll have to resign your commission? I'm sorry, Chas. You were a fine soldier."

Charles threw off his robe and stepped into his small clothes then his breeches. Spec handed him his linen shirt and he put it on, tucked it into the waistband.

Having spent much of the last three years together under conditions which could best be described as 'hellish,' Spec leapt to his captain's defense. "The finest," Spec vowed. "Your 'darling brother' led the bayonet charge at Busaco. We killed at least seventy Frenchmen that day, eh, Captain? Hold still while I tie this."

Expelling a breath of air which moved the long hair off his forehead, Charles stood as patiently as he could while Spec arranged his neck cloth. It irked, having lost so much dexterity in his hand that he couldn't do these simple tasks himself. But he still insisted on shaving himself. Having been on the working end of a rapier, Charles couldn't tolerate anyone near him with a straight blade. For the same reason, he hadn't suffered having his hair cut since the November battle and it now skimmed past his collar.

"That number seems to swell in your memories, Spec. As I recall, we managed to nick three foot soldiers and one lieutenant before I received this scratch and your leg got in the way of that musket ball." Charles lifted his damaged hand then pointed at his valet's busted knee.

"Hah!" Spec said.

"It looks like a wilted flower," Charles glared at his valet, whose knowledge in tying cravats surpassed his loose grip on the King's English.

Spec defended, "It's called a Problematical."

"The term is 'Mathematical,'" Charles snapped. Craning his neck, he inspected the result in the looking glass and determined, "But after seeing this, I think your term's more accurate."

"Ignoring your flagrant lies and Spec's exaggerations," Will continued, speaking over their squabbling. "What troubles you about losing the title of captain? I could have sworn you weren't that keen to remain in the war."

"It's not that. I'm unsure if I can be as good a 'gentleman farmer' as I've been an Army captain. The only thing I know is how to be a soldier. Acting as a father is new business for me and I don't relish the learning curve." Charles strolled to where his brother sat and sipped from Will's cup of coffee. "I'm in no condition to travel today. Will you delay your return to London?"

"Certainly. We can journey down next week. I'll write to inform Mama of the change in plans." Will took back his coffee and drank it, ignoring his brother's protest and telling him to get his own cup.

"Good. The nursery's nearly ready, having already been painted—"

"When do you plan to meet Arianna, darling brother?" Will's butter-wouldn't-melt-in-his-mouth expression made Charles leery.

"Soon." His words were clipped as he returned to the original topic. "I've had her room painted pink. Will she enjoy that, do you think?"

"How should I know?"

"You know her better than I," Charles pointed out.

"Pink's fine." The earl gave a dismissive wave.

"Good."

"With you selling out your commission, it's time to make permanent arrangements for your daughter. Mama would be willing, I'm sure, to interview governesses and hire one for your daughter."

"Oh?" Charles inquired, massaging his hand. It did trouble him this morning.

"Spec?" The earl called. "I believe Charles requires that unguent for his hand. Fetch it, please."

"Thank you," Charles murmured.

Charles flexed his hand, cursing the stiffness. Busaco occurred months ago. He expected his hand to be healed by now; so, too, had Dr. Chandler. 'If you haven't recovered full mobility by now, you never will,' he'd pronounced last week in his London office. Right before the nodcock addressed him by his civilian title, not his army rank.

"Would Mama be willing to undertake that duty?"

"I'm sure she will. Such things are in her bailiwick."

"Should I ask Mama to live at Kedington? I don't wish to separate her from the girl if it would cause either one pain."

Will's coffee cup clattered to the saucer. "The *girl* is your daughter. Why is it so difficult for you to say that?"

Charles glowered at his brother, but Will disregarded it, as is the privilege of the eldest sibling.

"You're more father than uncle to Arianna. Having spent four years in the 48th Foot, I don't even know what Vivian's child looks like."

Carrying a jar of foul-smelling unguent, Spec re-entered. As impudent as he was efficient, he'd already removed the lid. Charles rubbed the mix into his hand.

"That smells awful, Chas! Go stand over there." Will pointed to the window.

Charles laughed, but did so.

"May we speak privately, darling brother?"

Charles' dark eyebrows lifted, but after glancing toward Spec noted his former batman had already begun to leave the room.

"I'll be in the kitchens."

Once the door shut behind him, Charles inquired, "What's this?"

Will steepled his hands together, taking his time to speak. "Have you ever considered re-marrying, Chas?"

Charles shuddered. "Lord, no! Being made a cuckold once is more than enough."

"I never cared for Vivian, but not all women are unfaithful. Why not come to London and search for a bride?"

"No," Charles said, slicing his hand through the air.

A silence descended over the brothers as Will poured himself another cup of coffee. He cleared his throat and said, "Your injuries made me realize two things. The first is that my younger brother may prove to be mortal, something I've never considered." Charles attempted to interrupt, but his brother waved him to silence. "The second is that it falls to you to continue the Dryden line. You need to sire an heir for the Earldom."

"No." Charles' repugnance sounded in his rapid repudiation. "Do not ask it of me again. I did marry—miserable wretch that she was—to please the family. I fought for my country. I even accepted—" He stopped the flow of his hot, angry words by pressing his lips together. "No."

Will softly said, "You must."

Something in those two simple, clipped words caused Charles' head to snap up. He despised whatever it was even if he couldn't name it. "Why the hell should I?"

The earl lifted one bony shoulder. "Because I cannot."

Charles stood by the open window. The breeze lifted the ends of his Problematical as a sense of inevitability began to suffocate him. Knowing how well Will had discharged the duties of the earldom since their father's passing, it escaped Charles how his brother could fail in this essential task. Frowning, he wondered what Will meant.

"I've not the stomach for the act." Will's gaze slid past him, as if he couldn't bring himself to look him in the eye.

Charles' brain juggled to comprehend what Will meant. "Are you…healthy?"

"Yes."

That left another possibility, one which was a hanging offense. Tilting his head, he recalled the times without number young ladies failed to capture Will's eye. Had he mistaken his brother's disinterest for restraint? Apparently so. "Huh."

"Are you all right?"

Typical that Will would ask after him. Charles smiled to reassure him. "I am. Are you?"

A bolt lanced through Charles as he witnessed his brother's struggle to maintain composure. In three easy strides, he crossed the room to give Will a quick, fierce, back-slapping hug.

After a while, Will cleared his throat then spoke, "You see now why it's imperative for you to remarry and provide the world with an heir."

Charles returned to the window, inhaling deeply. Lord, he'd quelled at the idea of becoming a gentleman farmer, and being a father to Arianna. On top of those two Herculean tasks, he must become a husband again? He closed his eyes. It was too much.

"Can you not…marry anyway? There are several cuckoos in various nests within the *Beau Monde*."

"You'd wish the next Lord Northampton to have no drop of Dryden blood?" Will shuddered. "I think not."

Of course Charles didn't wish to have their family lineage obliterated from the pages of history. The Earldom was an ancient title. He sighed, mourning the near-empty decanter on his bedside table. If they must discuss marriage, he didn't want to do it sober.

"Hell and blast." He picked up the decanter and drank its entire contents.

"Give the matter some thought."

Charles flopped backward onto the bed and groaned.

Not put off by this theatrical display, Will approached his brother, grinning as he leaned over to ask, "Tell me, if you found a girl who could be faithful to you, would you marry her?"

"You and your hypothetical questions."

"No. Really. Consider it, Chas."

"Is she platter-faced, this hypothetical woman of yours? How else could I be assured of her faithfulness?" Charles scrunched his nose in disgust.

Will whistled. "Vivian really did you a disservice, but no, I'm sure your bride will, undoubtedly, be attractive."

An image of a silver-haired harridan popped into his thoughts. He'd been attracted to the silver icicle. Definitely attracted.

"Aha!" Charles waggled his finger at his brother. "Then she can't be the faithful sort."

"There's no use discussing this."

"None," Charles agreed with so much cheeriness in his tone that it solicited another one of Will's open grins.

Before departing the room, Will turned to him. "There *is* another reason to re-marry."

Charles lifted up on his elbows and waited.

Smiling broadly, Will said, "I received another picture from Arianna before traveling here. She draws beautifully."

Lifting his brow, he waited for an explanation.

"Yes, well, Arianna drew a picture of her, Juju, and the dolly I gave her at Christmas. They were having a tea party."

"Yes, so what's terrible about that?"

"Miss Lucille was frowning."

"Who the devil is Miss Lucille?"

"That's the name of Arianna's dolly."

Charles didn't know what to make of this tidbit. His brother waited with an air of expectation, but Charles could only stare blankly.

"If Miss Lucille's unhappy, then Arianna is, too."

Will's kernel of wisdom dropped into the small drawing room with the force of Napoleon's Imperial Guard.

"But to *re-marry*?" Charles made no effort to hide the dismay in his voice. Reclining, Charles threw an arm over his eyes to block out the sunshine. He sighed then waved his hand toward his brother. "Sometimes there's a great deal of sense in what you say, Will. Blind squirrel and all that."

"You overwhelm me, darling brother," Lord Northampton said before letting himself out.

Chapter 4

Winnie paused on the sidewalk outside the black iron fencing. She checked the newspaper advertisement to ensure she had the correct address: 44 Curzon Street, Hampton House. Two white columns made of marble flanked a handful of steps, which led to the front door. Above the lintel was a window shaped like a seashell. The house was tall. So tall that Winnie, craning her head as far as she could, still could not count its stories. At each floor, small balconies flanked the front corners. The iron fencing matched the street-level railing. Hampton House must belong to a mighty aristocrat. A Duke, perhaps?

Winnie recalled her home with its patched roof and peeling paint. Stanhope felt very distant.

Focusing on the brass knocker, which was shaped like a lion's head, she swallowed hard. A thrill of excitement, of embarking on a grand adventure, fizzed through her veins…until a sobering thought occurred. On this side of the front door, stood Winsome Montgomery, daughter of a deceased baronet, and member of the gentry. Once she crossed this threshold, she lost whatever status her father's title bestowed upon her.

She made a silent prayer: *When my father reaches the pearly gates, would you please scold him, St. Peter, for raiding my dowry?*

Her answer came swiftly. The phrase, 'Needs must when the devil drives,' popped into her head.

Gathering her courage, she lifted the brass knocker. It fell with a low clatter, which startled her frayed nerves. She chided herself for being a ninny.

The door opened before she could flee.

"Yes?" A butler, dressed in somber shades of gray, waited for her to state her business.

She wondered if she shouldn't have come to the back door as regular tradespeople did. Was a governess considered a tradesman? If this house belonged to a duke, she must address him as 'your Grace.' The wheels in her brain whirled, trying to remember all the rules of social etiquette her mother drilled into her before her early demise.

The sound of a throat clearing brought her back to attention.

"Yes, I've come to inquire regarding the position as governess. I am Winsome Montgomery."

He stepped back and motioned for her to enter. Taking a deep breath, she crossed the great divide, moving from gentry to servant with a single step.

Inwardly, she quaked. Maybe outwardly, as well. She could scarce attend as she was much struck with the elegance of this mansion.

Whatever Winnie had expected—and to be fair, she hadn't given the matter much thought—it wasn't this. Checking her stride, she was overwhelmed by magnificence. Her gaze slewed skyward. The ornate plaster medallion centered on the painted ceiling was surrounded by a replica of Michelangelo's masterpiece where God touched Adam with the Divine Spark. A colorful tapestry adorned the wall, providing warmth and muffling traffic noises.

Stanhope, her beloved but destitute home, seemed far away.

The butler bowed, and intoned, "Please wait a moment while I inquire of the countess."

Countess? So this was an earl's residence? Winnie made a jerky nod, her nerves getting the better of her. No need to address her as 'your Grace.' Just 'my lady,' or 'your ladyship,' as the case may be.

Winnie wiped a sweaty palm against her skirts. She finger-combed her hair into some order. Self-conscious that she lacked a bonnet and gloves, she wished her new dress weren't so plain. After insisting the Dobson's take half of the windfall, she had splurged, purchasing a new pair of shoes and a practical dress which buttoned down the front. Remembering her initial delight in having a new outfit, her cheeks heated with embarrassment. Her entire ensemble cost twelve shillings. Without a stranger's generosity, she wouldn't even have that much. Standing amidst this luxurious decor, she felt as awkward as a duck in a parade of swans.

She cast a longing glance toward the outer door as the butler's footsteps faded. Once she gained her solitude, Winnie forced herself to take deep, calming breaths. She flexed her good hand, closing her eyes.

"Don't be a ninny, Winnie." The rhyme made her smile and if she weren't so nervous, she might have laughed.

Her lids fluttered open and she stood before the tapestry. Cowering beneath brush, wedged between the roots of a very large tree, a fox hunkered. Without thinking, Winnie's fingertips touched the threads of its copper coat, smoothing what would have been its coat. She whispered to herself, "I hope you make it, Mr. Fox, and live another day."

"How did you know his name?"

Winnie snatched her hand from the tapestry, surprised to find the uplifted face of a four-year old girl staring at her.

She carried on in a matter-of-fact voice. "Well, of course he's Mr. Fox. Who else could he be?"

Round eyes blinked as the girl's finger disappeared into her mouth. She waited to hear what the ninny would say next.

Smiling at that thought, Winnie improvised, "Mr. Fox is clearly a respectable family man who enjoys out-witting the hounds, but finds himself in a tight spot. His wife, a brave, saucy little vixen, will have to rescue him." Squinting at the hunt scene, Winnie pointed to a distant orange speck. "There's Mrs. Fox's tail. She's making her way toward her husband."

"How?"

"By tunneling, I imagine." She peered closer at the tapestry. "Here it is—do you see this channel?"

"Where?"

"Right here. She's made an opening to a tunnel so Mr. Fox can escape."

"Oh." The girl pressed her nose against the tapestry, her hands spread wide. She pointed to the lead dog, bearing down on the poor fox. Its jowls hanged half-open, his tongue and mouth glistened with anticipatory moisture as it readied for the kill. "What's his name?"

The name, 'Sir David' popped into Winnie's head, but she replied, "Meanie. Mean old' Mr. Meanie. That suits him, don't you think?"

The girl's finger, disappearing again, hooked on the bottom lip of a wet, sloppy grin.

"I am Miss Montgomery. It's a pleasure to meet you."

The girl swiveled her hips, allowing her skirts to swing about her. "Miss Mont-gumphrey?"

"Montgomery," Winnie said with a smile. "It *is* quite a mouthful, isn't it? If you like, you may call me Miss Monty."

After giving the adult a long, thorough inspection, Arianna announced, "My name is Arianna. You're very pretty, Miss Monty."

She murmured her thanks, grateful the child hadn't developed a fashion sense yet, or else she might, like the female pedestrian outside, have thought otherwise.

Arianna gestured to Winnie's broken arm. "Does your arm hurt?"

"A bit," Winnie lied. "I broke it, and now must carry it in this sling until it heals."

"Oh." The little girl faced the tapestry again, pointing at it. "Tell me more, please."

Searching her brain for some amusing tale, Winnie pointed to one of the red-coated riders. "That is Sir Alfred—quite the athlete. Considered to be a bruising rider, a real top-sawyer."

A headful of blonde curls bounced as she nodded her understanding. "A Co-co-ring-then."

"Corinthian," Winnie corrected as her lips quirked with a ready laugh. She pointed to another figure in the scene. "This man is the jolly squire. He and his wife allow their dogs to roam inside their country house. Never having children of their own, the Squire and Mrs. Wigglesbottom spoil their dogs by feeding them ginger biscuits."

"Gingerbread men?"

"No, no. Only *people* eat gingerbread men. The Wigglesbottom's dogs love ginger biscuits shaped like *bones*."

The two giggled.

"Miss Montgomery, Lady Northampton will meet you now."

"Very good. Thank you, sir." Winnie glanced at her young companion. "Before I leave, I must tell you that you are very pretty, too, Arianna. Goodbye."

"Goodbye, Miss Monty."

Winnie peeked over her shoulder, glimpsing Arianna's shining face and her soggy wave 'goodbye.'

Hope rose within her breast upon viewing the sunny countenance. Perhaps life as a governess wouldn't be a hardship, after all.

***

A week later, Winnie thanked her lucky stars the Countess of Northampton had hired her. She'd sailed close to the wind, judging from the way Lady Northampton boggled at her demands. Recalling her audacity when the offer came made Winnie shiver.

"I'm sure your son is an honorable man, my lady." Winnie stammered out the lie. She had no idea who Charles Dryden was, let alone whether he was honorable or not. "Not having known many honorable men, however, I hesitate to place my livelihood at a stranger's discretion. I'll accept the post with the condition that he cannot discipline or fire me. Nor is he to make lewd advances and if he does, I shall not answer to the consequences."

Lady Northampton whistled, something Winnie was certain the proper and correct countess rarely, if ever, did.

"My son does not take advantage of the help, Miss Montgomery. He was raised better than that and knows what is due his name." The countess' arctic tones didn't bode well.

Winnie gazed at the tips of her new shoes, miserable for having blundered this opportunity. She argued with herself, how else could she be certain she wasn't leaping from the frying pan into the fire? Neither the countess nor her son—whoever he was— were known to her.

"What's the remedy if you prove to be unsatisfactory?" Lady Northampton asked.

"I won't," Winnie vowed, glad the lady proved willing to talk rather than summarily ordering her to leave Hampton House. "However, if *you* feel I am not working out to your satisfaction, then naturally you should fire me and I'll abide by that decision."

Tapping her fingers on the arm rest, Lady Northampton's eyes narrowed upon her, but Winnie straightened her shoulders and met the widow's gaze. After several long moments of contemplation, a slight smile crept across the countess' lips. She stood, extended her hand to Miss Montgomery, and offered her the position and yearly salary of £28.

Winnie Montgomery blinked then surged upright, grasping the woman's hand and shaking it with great enthusiasm. Twenty-eight pounds was a veritable fortune!

The first week of employment passed. On the whole, Winnie was happy with her room in the attic. Its mattress was without lumps and she had a fluffy pillow. The roof didn't leak. Being an upper servant at Hampton House was a holiday compared to being mistress of Stanhope.

Her charge, Arianna, was a certifiable chatterbox and utterly delightful. Sometimes Winnie watched, amazed, at the girl's rapidly moving mouth, delighted to be privy to her tales. Before several days passed, Winnie wished she could claim the girl as her own. While the idea of not marrying didn't disturb Winnie one whit, she found that the idea of never being a mother did.

Such was a governess' lot.

Winnie was astonished to learn Arianna's father had returned from the war several months ago, yet remained at Hampton House only a fortnight. Charles Dryden saw the earl's physician then high-tailed to his estate, Kedington, where he now resided.

One day, out of Arianna's hearing, Winnie asked Juju, the nanny, "Why hasn't the captain sent for his daughter?"

"Oh, I 'pect Kedington needs his full attention."

Winnie arched her brow. "More than his daughter?"

"You know how men are," Juju shrugged. Having been the nanny for the earl and Mr. Dryden, her fondness for the two brothers was clear in the bedtime stories she'd tell Arianna of their childhood adventures. She also embellished her father's wartime exploits into tales of daring so that whenever Arianna spoke of Mr. Dryden, her eyes gleamed with pride.

"Arianna adores her father, doesn't she?"

Juju grinned. "Yes. He's a handsome man and just as handsome in his manners."

"But he's been absent from her life, saving for his short, recent visit to London."

"Aye, but he always remembered her in his letters back home."

"Such exertion."

Juju's head jerked toward her. After a considerable silence, the African woman patted her hand and assured Winnie, "Don't worry. He and the earl will return next week. Once you know him, you'll like Charles."

On Friday afternoon, Winnie and Arianna returned from strolling in the park to find the earl's carriage outside Hampton House. Squealing with delight, Arianna tugged Winnie's hand as they crossed the distance, weaving through pedestrians. When they were close, she wrenched free of Winnie's hold and ran into her uncle's outstretched arms. "Uncle Will! Uncle Will! Oh, I missed you!"

"I missed you, too, poppet." He lifted her and planted a kiss on her cheek.

She began informing her uncle of all the things she'd learned, how well behaved she'd been, that they'd discovered a mama duck and her baby ducks at the park, that baby ducks are so funny—doesn't he think so?

Throughout Arianna's babbling, Lord Northampton listened in rapt attention with an indulgent smile.

"Where's my papa?" Arianna squirmed in the earl's embrace, vainly trying to spot the stranger who claimed to be her father.

"He remains at Kedington, preparing the home for you. Said he wants your room painted so that everything is just right."

"Oh." She put her finger into her mouth.

"Arianna, please take your hand from your mouth. There's a good girl," Winnie said. She curtsied to the earl and introduced herself. "I am Miss Montgomery, Arianna's new governess."

"Good day, miss." Lord Northampton bowed.

"I believe Arianna has made several drawings for you, my lord."

"Excellent. I have a keen sense of artistry and look forward to seeing your interpretations, niece."

Arianna nodded, her uncle's facetious comment sailing past her. "I know some of my A, B, C's, Uncle Will."

"You do?"

She nodded again.

Winnie laughed at Arianna's earnest expression and touched the top of her hair. "It's a pity Captain Dryden hasn't accompanied you. I intended to give him a progress report concerning Arianna."

At the earl's quizzical look, Winnie hastened to add, "My mother required the same from my governesses on a weekly basis."

"Oh." His brow cleared. "Well, by all means, you should do so. I shall provide his direction and you may write your report to him. I'll frank the postage."

That certainly didn't sound like Captain Dryden would be coming to London soon. Winnie shook her head.

The earl must have read her expression because he added, "Charles is avoiding London to thwart Mama's matchmaking tendencies, I suspect."

"Oh. So he has no wish to remarry?"

"None whatsoever."

"Thank you, my lord, for offering to send my reports to him. I suppose it's best to communicate this way, given his understandable reluctance to return to London."

Lady Northampton greeted her eldest as the trio entered Hampton House.

"Mama! How splendid you look." The earl greeted his parent.

"Thank you, William. Has Charles chosen to remain at Kedington then? What a shame! I've met the Misses Stanleys and Lady Genevieve, all of whom I thought—well, never mind what I thought." The countess' voice cooled by the time she'd reached the end of her speech.

"He thought it best to remain so that he could hire additional staff." Northampton winked at Winnie, his expression one of 'I-told-you-so.'

He shifted Arianna's weight in his arms and spoke to his niece "Also, he wished to refurbish the nursery and schoolroom for his daughter."

"Does Charles plan to come to town later?" the countess asked.

"In due time, I imagine. By the by, he's sold out his commission, so the appellation 'captain' will probably only be used by his valet, Spec."

Lady Northampton shuddered. "That fellow."

"Now, Mama. There's nothing wrong with Spec."

"He always misusing his words, putting on airs," she protested.

The earl set Arianna on the marble floor then guided her back into Winnie's care, gesturing by a jerk of his head that he expected her to lead the girl away. He addressed his mother. "But that's his charm, ma'am!"

Winnie and Arianna returned to the nursery, washed up, then shared their evening meal. Once that was finished, Winnie brushed Arianna's hair then put the girl to bed. Juju had instilled good habits and so without being prodded, Arianna knelt beside her bed and began her nightly prayers. She included her uncle, grandmamma, and papa. She asked for blessings on Juju and Miss Monty and Molly, the upstairs maid. And the baby ducks. And their ducky mama.

At last concluded with her long-winded requests, she climbed into bed.

Winnie cracked the window, allowing a gentle night breeze into the nursery. She returned to Arianna's bed to press a kiss on her forehead when her unusual stillness communicated something was wrong.

"What is it, dear?"

Arianna's finger popped into her mouth. "Papa."

"Yes? What about him? Are you disappointed he didn't arrive with your uncle?"

She clutched her blanket. "How will he know what color to paint my room if I don't tell him?"

"Yes, I see what you mean. That *is* a problem. What color would you wish?"

Arianna wrinkled her forehead, giving the matter serious consideration before finally deciding. "Green. Like the leaves on the trees in the park."

"I shall write to your papa and advise him of your preference," Winnie promised, not sure if Mr. Dryden would grant the wish or not. He'd already displayed a callous disinterest in his daughter. She wouldn't be surprised if he disregarded Arianna's wishes in this small matter. That would fit the character of a neglectful father.

Nevertheless, Winnie wrote a letter to her employer.

Mr. Dryden, if it pleases you, Arianna prefers a leaf-green bedroom. If you are unable to accommodate this wish, would you please send measurements for the window? I shall be happy to sew curtains for her room, at my own expense, naturally. Your daughter is an energetic, intelligent little girl. On an outing today in the park, she held a newborn duckling in her palm, giggling as its downy feathers tickled her chin. I have begun to teach her the alphabet and she is eager to learn, absorbing new experiences with relish.
Signed,
Miss Montgomery, Governess to Arianna.

Uncertain whether Lady Northampton had informed her son of her name, Winnie added the last three words for Mr. Dryden's benefit so that he wouldn't think her presumptuous.

A week later, having received no response, Winnie wrote another letter.

Mr. Dryden, Arianna is eager to see her bedchambers at Kedington and the other improvements you've been busy making to the house and estate. If you require anything from London to outfit the schoolroom, please send me a list so that I may procure those items. You may either reimburse me for the costs later or allow me to charge against your credit. Please advise. Arianna plays well with other children and is very considerate when handling the duckies. She can recite the alphabet, with few mistakes. I read to her daily and she asks if you are soldiering in Kedington. It may well be time for her to learn a bit of geography.
Signed,
Miss Montgomery, Arianna's Governess

Disappointed by Mr. Dryden's non-response, Winnie skipped the next weekly report. Two weeks passed that she sent another letter.

Mr. Dryden, I'm happy to report that Arianna knows her colors, shapes, and alphabet. We have begun botany and geography lessons, focusing foremost on English matters, but she's eager to learn of the Iberian Peninsula. Her uncle has hinted a pony awaits her at Kedington. She is very anxious to meet it and to see you again, sir. Please tell me when I may bring her to Kedington—she is most eager to be there! Now that the ducks have grown, she seeks another outlet for her affections.
Your daughter's governess, Miss Montgomery

Winnie was mystified by Mr. Dryden's continued silence. She did not think it improper to correspond with her employer regarding his child's progress. If pressed, Winnie could confess she hoped Mr. Dryden might be nettled to show a bit more care toward his daughter, but never did it occur to her the letters could be misconstrued as giving offense.

It's true, Juju, the nursemaid, found them highly entertaining, but the woman shook her head and clucked her tongue when Winnie pressed her to explain her amusement. But then, Juju was always grinning about something.

When the countess informed Winnie her son wished them to travel to Canon Ashby so that he could collect Arianna there and bring her to Kedington, Winnie sarcastically remarked to Juju she was relieved to discover the former captain could write at all.

The African woman roared with laughter upon hearing Winnie's less-than-gracious remark. Accustomed to Juju's odd sense of humor, Winnie no longer bothered to ask why she laugh.

Sitting in the well sprung carriage, a much smoother ride than the mail coach from Stanhope to London, Winnie stared out the window as Arianna rested her head in her lap. She toyed with Arianna's blonde hair, luxuriating in its soft curls.

"Will Mr. Dryden have already arrived at Canon Ashby?" Winnie asked while Arianna slept.

"Yes. He avoided London, as I should have predicted. Defiant and stubborn, that's Charles." She shrugged. "Side-stepping the parson's mouse trap, I believe, by not coming in the vicinity of any eligible miss."

"Do you think so?"

"Oh yes. Charles doesn't wish to re-marry." She glanced at Winnie. "He's a good, decent man. I'm sure the two of you will rub along well."

Echoing a polite, but futile hope, Winnie turned her face from Lady Northampton's then clamped her lips together, angry with fathers who failed to appreciate their daughters.

Chapter 5

Canon Ashby, outside Culworth, England

Charles stood on the wide steps of Canon Ashby, his feet planted on the pebble drive, shoulder-width apart, with his hands clasped behind his back. His carriage was ramrod straight, assuming the customary pose of the military man as he awaited his brother's traveling coach. The earl had already arrived, minutes earlier, on horseback to alert the household of the pending arrival. The carriage pulled up, scattering gravel in its wake. A footman set the steps down as Lord Northampton, brushing off his travel dust, came to stand beside his brother to greet their parent.

Breaking into a smile, Charles assisted his mother from the carriage. "How are you, Mama? You look well, I see."

She kissed his cheek. "Thank you, my dear. It's so good to see you again. I hope Mrs. Halstead's prepared tea for us. I'm famished!"

Charles smiled as he ushered her toward the stone steps of Canon Ashby. "I believe Cook has anticipated your needs."

"Papa!"

He faced the girl whose eyes reminded him of her mother. With her arms outstretched Arianna greeted him, but in her exuberance, she flung herself from the carriage. Charles half-dove, managing to grasp her pinafore in a mad scramble, but his grip didn't have its usual strength. The material slipped through his injured hand and she tumbled to the ground.

"Arianna! I'm so so—"

Her bright blue gaze stabbed him.

51

Charles knew how Judas must have felt.

Arianna clutched her skinned knees, whimpering.

He stood over her, helpless.

It was her uncle Will who scooped her up and soothed her.

As she clung to his brother, Charles castigated himself. In all his years as a soldier, he'd never let down his regiment, but he'd bungled matters with Arianna. He tried to speak, but words failed. His hand throbbed and his chest tightened.

With her finger in her mouth, she peeked at him beneath wet, spiky lashes.

Good Lord.

His mother called to her. "Come, Arianna, and let us tend your injuries."

Grateful for his mother's assistance, Charles watched the girl limp into the house. He closed his eyes, cursing his clumsiness. He repressed a sigh, turning to help the governess from the coach then blinked twice.

The young woman gazed downward as she exited the carriage, her eyelashes casting crescent shadows upon her smooth cheeks. In one hand she carried a basket; the other arm was in a sling. Her straw bonnet was askew as she clambered down the steps.

Recognizing the silver-haired icicle from Bannock's Inn, Charles' heart made a joyful leap. That same heart sank he recalled she'd declared him the stupidest person she'd ever met. Given her spat of condescending letters, it was apparently the shrew's opinion hadn't changed.

Her gaze locked with his and her eyes widened.

"You!" She reared backward, falling against the coach steps.

His bad day just got worse.

"Lord! I'm not Beelzebub, woman." He grabbed her by the healthy elbow and pulled her upright, out of reason cross.

Her knees buckled and he tightened his grip, worried she'd collapse. Should he assist her up the step, stuff her inside the carriage, and order the driver to spring the horses? The idea appealed…

In an angry undertone he warned, "Don't speak until we are private."

She stepped away, giving him an opportunity to observe her appearance. Both her color and collar were high— unflatteringly so. The smooth cheeks were splotchy, hued with the stain of mortification while her skirts were darned and her cuffs were frayed. She looked as discombobulated as he felt.

"I beg your pardon." Charles' apology surprised himself; he rarely apologized.

Miss Montgomery made a sharp, disdainful nod.

Heaving a sigh, he dashed his hands through his hair, aware his brother had witnessed their debacle of a reunion. Charles glowered at Will until he grimaced then entered Canon Ashby.

By the time Charles' gaze swung toward her, the governess had retrieved a battered basket from the stack of luggage the coachman was piling on the pebble drive. He recognized her makeshift portmanteau, having lugged it before. Annoyed for a myriad of reasons, none of which he could articulate, he tugged the basket from her.

"I can carry it."

"No, you won't!"

Miss Montgomery blinked in astonishment.

Charles inhaled, praying for immediate patience. "Allow me to perform this courtesy. It would be my pleasure."

"Oh. Certainly, sir." She paused, as if recalling her own manners then continued, "I am Miss Montgomery, the governess for Arianna."

Finally. She'd given him her name.

"Charles Dryden, at your service," he said.

She colored again, picking up on his rueful tone. "Thank you for your assistance, Mr. Dryden."

It was the first civil thing she'd said to him. Giddy with the progress, he rushed straight into idiocy. "When do you expect the rest of your luggage, ma'am?"

He realized his mistake by the fierce tilt of her chin.

Stiffly, she replied, "I have nothing else, sir."

So, Miss Montgomery had more prickly pride than worldly possessions. Glimpsing her frayed cuffs, he wondered if her worldly goods were as humble as her wardrobe.

Marveling at his knack for discomforting her, Charles felt the desire to be elsewhere, perhaps at the front where there would be shooting. "Once you have washed off your traveling dust, Miss Montgomery, please report to me. A footman will guide you to the study. Will thirty minutes give you enough time to prepare?"

"Yes, sir."

"Very well."

He gave the basket to a footman and instructed the man to escort Miss Montgomery to her room. With a small nod, he left her.

Charles searched out his mother, determined to find the architect of this catastrophic hiring decision. Long strides and sharp footfalls brought him to his mother's chambers, but before he could berate her, she spun from the wash basin.

Tossing a hand towel aside, she beamed at him as she rushed across the room. "Charles, it's so delightful to see you! You mustn't worry about Arianna—she'll be fine. Now, come. Show me your hand. Has it healed?"

Galled that he couldn't quarrel with a solicitous woman, he tugged off his glove. He'd forgotten his mama would make a fuss. Of course she'd make a fuss.

"I wore the glove so that I wouldn't frighten Arianna," he explained. "It looks terrible."

The countess' gaze fastened onto his injury with the same clinical assessment he'd observed in the field hospital or the private physician Will insisted he visit. She skimmed her hand across the pink scar where his finger should have been.

"Hmm," she said, frowning. "I suspect you'll regain some of the movement. Have you been using a mustard-based poultice, massaging it in several times a day?"

"Spec mixes an unguent, but I've no idea what's in it."

"I'll have Mrs. Collins prepare a comfrey, shall I? And you really must insist your valet give you a haircut. I'm sure he's not an ideal barber, but if there's someone else you'd prefer…"

54

"Thank you, Mama," he said, having no intention of allowing anyone to approach him with a blade. "As to the governess—"

She clapped her hands. "Isn't she wonderful? It was a real stroke of brilliance on my part, if I say so. Adrianna simply adores her! As does Juju, which is, by no means, a small feat."

Firing Miss Montgomery was not an option. Not unless he wished to anger his mama, former nanny, and Arianna. He'd sooner face a firing squad.

His mother studied her reflection, patting her hair into place. "She comes from a good family—her father was a baronet, Sir Vernon Montgomery. Have you heard of him? No? Well, he recently died in the Fleet. Gambling debts, did you know that?"

"Her father was an impoverished baronet?"

"Mm-hmm."

"Was there no one to take her in?"

The countess shrugged. "She hasn't spoken of it, and I don't wish to pry. I'm not one to gossip."

"Never." Charles' mouth twitched.

"Charles." His mother cleared her throat, averting her gaze elsewhere. A sneaky suspicion warned him he would not like what his mother would say.

"Yes, Mama?"

"Before agreeing to take the post, Miss Montgomery placed two conditions upon her employment. They were reasonable requests, but unconventional. I can only imagine the horrors which drove her to seek them. Having left Arianna in my care since birth, I hope you don't think I overstepped my authority?"

Her question wasn't really a question, he noted. The Countess of Northampton had developed a handy little habit whenever she'd landed in a sticky situation. His father had long lamented it, but his adored wife would choose to seek forgiveness rather than permission in order to achieve her ends. It was a marvelously effective method for driving a husband mad, and even better for getting what she wanted.

"What have you done, ma'am?"

"I agreed to Miss Montgomery's terms."

Her shrug—so practiced, so nonchalant—didn't fool Charles a whit. He refused to speak, tactically allowing her to fill the pregnant silence.

"Yes. The first condition's teensy-tiny. Hardly of note. In the normal run of things, I view it as a domestic concern. Not your line at all."

His brow arched, but he held his tongue and his patience. Whatever it was his mother agreed to must be egregious. The intensity of his stare communicated itself to the countess and for the first time in their interview, she appeared uneasy. Her gaze flitted from his while she twitched the folds of her skirt.

"Mama."

"I agreed that I alone would have the authority to either discipline or terminate the governess."

Charles stared at her blankly. After a few moments, he shook his head in disbelief then politely inquired, "I beg your pardon, Mama, but for a moment I thought you say you would exert authority over my servant?"

"Oh, really, Charles. There's no need for sarcasm."

"Next you'll be telling me it's not a hanging offense you've committed, either."

"Hanging offense? Bah!"

He pinched the bridge of his nose, realizing the futility of arguing when his mother was in such a defensive state. "What was the second condition?"

"Umm…the second?"

Leveling another direct stare at her, her dismissive wave immediately set off the warning bells in his head.

"Oh, just the usual. What every female employee has a right to expect in any English household, I suppose."

"Good Lord, Mama, will you just spit it out?"

Again, there was that suspicious shrug. "I simply assured her you wouldn't make any lewd advances to her."

"WHAT?"

"Now don't be angry—"

"Angry? Oh, I'm not angry, Mama."

"You're not? I must say, you appear rather…out of sorts. There's a vein bulging in your neck."

She pointed at the spot, as if he didn't bloody well know where it was located.

"I'm incensed. Outraged. Appalled." He let each word fall from his tongue in a deliberate manner before rifling his hair. "I couldn't expect anything but plaguy treatment from *her*—" he nearly spat the word—"but from my own *mother*?"

"Now, now, Charles. It's not a betrayal—"

Slamming the door shut, he stomped away, prepared to battle the governess as if she were Marshal Massena at his last battle of Busaco.

***

"You wished to see me, sir?"

Charles Dryden had been studying his steward's report with such blistering intensity it was a wonder it hadn't ignited. His head jerked up as he spied the governess hovering on the threshold. Something else jerked up, too, forcing him to remain seated. "Excuse me for not rising," he said, straight-faced.

She took the chair opposite the desk with a deceptive air of timidity.

He knew she wasn't as demure as she appeared. The harridan he'd met at Bannock's hadn't been the least bit shy, and the letters she'd written were masterpieces in subtle chastisement for neglecting his daughter.

In her drab gown with its starched collar, she was the epitome of every eunuch's dream. Yet there was something appealing about her even though he couldn't name it. He cursed the quality, whatever it was. He reminded himself she was a shrew, that her skirts were so voluminous, she might very well be hiding hips as broad as a Ship of the Line. It would be just the kind of trick a harridan would play, disguising a monstrous figure so corpulent it could rival Prinny's.

There. That did the trick. He was no longer attracted to Miss Montgomery. She wasn't the least bit enticing, he assured himself.

"I didn't wish to reveal the circumstances of our initial meeting because it doesn't reflect well on either of us," he said.

"I was not drunk, gambling, and making up to the serving girl." She sniffed, a sound of disapproval which he immediately recognized and hated.

"That's not how I remembered it."

"What?" Her eyelids flew open.

Delighted to get a rise from the Silver Icicle, he said, "As I recall, you behaved like a sanctimonious snob, and had tippled from the whisky bottle."

Miss Montgomery shot straight from her chair. "That is not true!"

"Is, too!"

"Is not and I can prove it!"

"Fine." He encouraged her with a wave. "Go on."

Miss Montgomery lifted her forefinger and said, "First, I was not *tippling*. I do not *tipple*."

Given the amount of scorn she injected into the verb, he had no other choice but to believe her.

"Recall my arm is broken. Traveling caused it to ache prodigiously, so I took a capful of laudanum, which was a reasonable amount, but because the *serving girl didn't bother* to bring me a glass of water, I was forced to drink it without and it tasted awful."

He squirmed at the mention of Fancy Nancy.

"My companion, Mrs. Sheridan, still had tea, so I drank it, discovering too late the lady wasn't drinking tea, but whisky." She arched her brows at him as she paused for breath.

He conceded that particular point; his sense of fairness demanded it, but he did so with ill grace.

"As to being displeased the coachman ignored his duties, I make no apology. He was derelict in his duty, as was the innkeeper. No wheelwright was summoned that evening, which delayed my journey by an entire day—a delay, sir, that I could ill afford."

"I suppose you blame me for that?"

"No, sir, I do not. So, I'm neither tippler nor snob," she concluded in a prim tone.

It dawned on Charles he was losing this debate. To avoid such an unhappy result, he launched an offensive.

"I don't think you've fully acquitted yourself of the charges of snobbery. Recall your revulsion for my damaged hand."

"Your wound doesn't repulse me."

Her look of bewilderment nearly convinced him she was sincere. Nearly, but not quite, for Charles wasn't a raw recruit. He made an irrefutable argument with a pithy disclaimer.

"Hah!"

"I'm not repulsed by your hand, sir. Nor was I ever. If you perceived my disgust—well, you're correct, but it was not for that reason I held you in contempt."

"Aha!" His triumph turned to dismay as he saw his shallow victory. Like Dogberry from "Much Ado About Nothing," wishing he'd been writ an ass.

"It was your shameless conduct—gambling, wenching, and drunkenness, that disgusted me. Not your hand. Never that." Her expression softened upon her last words.

He stared, unable to think of anything to say, which only added to his fury.

"When I met Lady Northampton, I didn't realize you were Arianna's father."

"Then why make those ridiculous conditions before accepting my offer of employment?"

"Ridiculous?"

He continued speaking over her indignant squawk. "Conditions which prove you rate my honor cheap."

"I assure you, Mr. Dryden, those precautions are quite necessary."

"Because you think me a gambler, womanizer, and—what was the last bit? Oh yes, drunkard."

"No, I believe I've already established that I did not piece your identity with that of Arianna's father at the time I accepted this post."

"You would have asked for those conditions, regardless of who your employer would be?" He allowed the lofty heights of his dark brows to reveal his skepticism.

"Yes, sir."

"You would have denied your employer the right to discipline you? Or terminate you? Forbidden them from making advances? Enlighten me, please, how anyone but my mother would have hired you, Miss Montgomery, given your impertinence?"

She clenched her jaw again, but he returned her topaz glare with one of his own. If Miss Montgomery thought she could insult his honor, he'd set her straight before another minute passed.

After a lengthy pause, the governess quizzed him. "Is it impertinent to demand I not be molested? Had I known of my employer's character, I might not have been so 'impertinent,' but again, Mr. Dryden, I didn't know you."

"Yet you assume I wouldn't have—"

She exploded, "What do you want me to say? If I *had* known your identity, I *would* have insisted on that onerous condition?" She gasped, covering her mouth too late to recall the words.

"Onerous? Onerous?"

Wild horses could drag him a hundred miles before he'd ever admit he once thought her attractive.

"You're under the mistaken impression that I find you either irresistible, convenient, or both. Let me assure you such isn't the case. You rate your attractions too high."

Even as he uttered the lie, he silenced the howling protests conjured within his brain and another vital body part.

After a few moments, he said, "It appears we're at an impasse. I can't fire you without confirming your worse prejudices. Nor would I want my mother to break her word."

"What do you propose?"

Her words were calm, but her face was quite pale.

Thinking on this, he ran the back of his knuckles across his desktop. He knocked once when he reached a solution. "I propose you do your job to the best of your abilities. Whenever we converse, our discussions will be brief and dispassionate. Agreed?"

She nodded.

Her pallor caused him consternation, which he shoved aside to inquire, "Tell me, Miss Montgomery, how goes Arianna?"

"Very well, sir."

"I had Arianna's bedchamber re-painted green." He offered, hoping to win a smile from her, forgetting his earlier rule of being dispassionate.

"Really?" Miss Montgomery beamed with pleasure.

When she smiled in that broad manner, her light blue eyes sparkled.

His lips curved in answer. "Yes. It was a reasonable request. Despite what you may think, I'm not an ogre, ma'am."

"She'll be happy to hear it, Mr. Dryden. Shall I send her into her papa now?"

"Not yet, my dear Miss Montgomery."

This next part was tricky. Given Vivian's string of affairs, Charles harbored doubts whether Arianna was his child. The girl was, after all, a stranger to him. Encouraging her affection felt dishonest. "You will have the girl address me as 'sir.' 'Papa' is not my preference, ma'am."

"Indeed, sir."

Gone was the warmth of the prior moment. The Silver Icicle was in full force as her topaz eyes turned as chilly as a winter's night. Miss Montgomery's jawbone tighten to an alarming degree and Charles had a passing concern for the condition of her teeth—that much grinding could be unhealthy.

"I am not your 'dear Miss Montgomery.'" The governess said, rearranging her skirts. "Nor shall I ever be, sir, so in future you would do well to refrain from addressing me as such."

Something in the way she uttered 'sir' robbed the title of its respect. Between her starched-up ways and her icy tones, Charles fought the urge to shake the shrew until her teeth rattled. He rearranged a few items on the top of his desk, taking special care not to touch the inkwell because his hands shook in anger.

The governess resumed the former thread of their conversation. "Arianna can write the alphabet, can identify shapes and colors. She enjoyed our outings in the park and I believe she has a very courageous heart."

"Ah, yes. The ducks. Impressive."

"Well, perhaps the family of ducks aren't so impressive, but your daughter certainly is. I mean to do my best to mold her into an intelligent, kind-hearted young lady." An earnest light came into those flashing eyes. Something akin to maternal pride, as odd as that seemed.

"What wages do I pay you, dear Miss Montgomery? Something tells me they are excessive."

"Twenty-eight pounds per annum, but having spent time with you, I suspect I'm underpaid," she muttered the last bit beneath her breath.

Miss Montgomery was a worthy opponent.

"Don't think to apply for more, my dear Miss Montgomery," he said with mock sternness.

"Perhaps I shall not, my lord, if you would be so kind as to address me in the preferred fashion I have already specified to you," she said between clenched teeth. "Shall we agree if, in the future, you address me as 'dear Miss Montgomery' then I shall receive additional compensation?"

"What?" Charles worried his jaw might scrape the desk top. Oh, that tail did love to wag the dog, didn't it?

"We could regard it as a fine, I suppose," she spoke in a helpful manner, mounting a blatant pretense.

She'd mastered the trick of widening her eyes so she'd project an image of innocence. God forbid she teach his daughter that! His fist came down hard on the desktop, upsetting the inkwell he'd lacked the foresight to relocate somewhere safer. It toppled over and spilled.

"Damnation! See what you've made me do?"

"What I made you do? What have I done?" Miss Montgomery's head turned left then right. She snatched a cloth, which rested close at hand and dabbed the mess as he held his papers aloft. Once the ink had been soaked up and the desk top cleaned through their combined efforts, he returned to the subject at hand as if there had been no interruption.

"I shall not pay a fine for addressing my employee as I see fit," he snarled.

"Then should we classify it as a tax?" A curious look came over her countenance. For the second time since meeting her, the corners of her mouth curved upward.

"Oh, dear. Um…in the rush…" She mumbled, "Not that you'll believe for one instant this was an accident—"

"What, pray, Miss Montgomery, are you mumbling about?" Then, looking at the ink-stained cloth in her hands, he understood her distress. "My shirt. You ruined my shirt!"

"Why was your shirt here anyway?" She fired back at him in accusatory tones.

Caught off-guard by her counter-attack, Charles snapped, "Because it lacked a button. I intended to deliver it to Mrs. Collins, the housekeeper."

"Oh."

"Quite."

"Your valet should be responsible for mending your clothes or carrying them to the housekeeper," she noted, unrepentant to her employer's increasing fury.

"You *ruined* my favorite shirt!"

With a sangfroid he envied, the governess coolly responded, "It appears so, sir."

Charles choked. The sizzle of anger which, moments before, rushed through him had transformed into something he recognized—desire. He made a sharp gesture toward the waste basket, inviting Miss Montgomery to deposit his shirt within it.

She did so without saying a word. That had to be a first.

"Do I amuse you, Miss Montgomery?"

"No, sir."

"I don't appear to have your undivided attention. Is it too much for ask for such courtesy while we hold a conversation?"

At the word 'courtesy,' Miss Montgomery's eyebrows snapped together. At his use of the term 'conversation,' her mouth gaped open.

Charles, fearing he would go into peals of unbridled, hysterical laughter, stood before the window where he could watch her expressions in the glass's reflection.

"How old are you?"

"Two-and-twenty," she ground out.

That surprised him.

Her eyes narrowed, taking in his start; an unintentional cut, but a cut nonetheless.

Well, he finally managed to vex her. He watched her jaw clench, certain he posed a threat to her dental health. He ran two fingers under his too-tight cravat. Bowing, he apologized, "I beg your pardon, ma'am."

But her eyes were not upon him. She missed his gracious gesture. Miss Montgomery remained seated, but her eyes closed as she massaged her arm. "It's of no consequence, sir."

Now he joined her in loathing himself. He'd made her arm throb. She probably had the headache, too. A pang shot through him and he approached her, hand extended in supplication. His next words, though, were greeted with astonishment by both occupants of the study. "Would you care for a glass of sherry? No, no. It's too early for that. Beg pardon. Perhaps a cup of chocolate or tea? A tisane? Laudanum?"

Her blue eyes widened.

With fear? He hoped not.

"N...no, thank you, sir."

Mortified, Charles clasped his hands and stared out the window. "Send Arianna in now, please."

Chapter 6

Dashing to her room, Winnie marveled her employer had taken offense at her conditions for employment. She was too riled to wonder why. Stomping up the stairwell, she fumed, recalling how he'd sat during the interview, all stiff and rigid, his dislike radiating toward her. What did it matter if Mr. Dryden disapproved of her? That wasn't her vanity chafing, surely?

She should be relieved—she *was* relieved. They mutually did not care for one another. Splendid. Excellent. Almost as splendid as his broad shoulders. Nearly as excellent as his well-formed legs.

A growl left her throat, startling herself.

She didn't find her employer attractive. Certainly, he possessed nice, broad shoulders. So what? Muscles had never rated that high with her, anyway, and his deep voice was probably caused by drinking too much.

"Hah!" she barked to no one as she entered her tiny room in the attic.

Across the barren plank flooring, she loudly stomped and picked up her mama's brush. She grimaced at her reflection in the window pane, slapping the silver-plated brush against her thigh. She looked as if she'd been dragged through the hedges. Bad enough a baronet's daughter should resemble the scullery maid, but the fall from her sphere to servitude made her want to weep. Knowing that a bout of crying would redden her nose and swell her eyes, she cursed instead, "Drat him!"

Winnie ripped off the despised spinster cap and brushed her short hair until it shone. Somewhat restored by that exercise, she returned the muslin and lace cap to its rightful place, suppressing her emotions. Covering her hair signaled either subservience or agedness and neither was particularly uplifting. She rammed it upon her head, tugged it into place, and ignored the involuntary whimper which escaped her pursed lips.

The image of an overturned inkwell formed in her mind's eye, making her grin. Recalling how she avenged herself—by sheer happenstance, although Mr. Dryden would never credit it—sent her into gales of laughter. She pictured his favorite shirt, lying in the bottom of the waste bin and her laughter blossomed into loud guffaws. Tears welled and her ribs ached, she laughed so hard.

Pressing her fingers against her lips, she pulled up short thinking of the final moments of their interview. Mr. Dryden became flustered, but why? She couldn't imagine a man of his address committing the *faux pas* of offering sherry to an upper servant before dinner. He'd seemed so…gobsmacked. His eyes boggled; his mouth gaped. She chuckled at the image.

At the height of his discomposure, though, a beam of sunlight rested upon him. It illuminated his wickedly handsome countenance, and the offer of sherry or laudanum struck her as kind. Winnie frowned, confused why Mr. Dryden could aggravate her one minute then be so endearing the next.

Angry with her herself, she mumbled, "'Tis nothing save a trick of lighting." She pulled her door shut with unnecessary vehemence, scolding herself for allowing Mr. Dryden's handsome face and athletic physique to make her forget he was a scoundrel. Like Sir David and her father, he was cut from the same bolt of scandal broth-scoundrel cloth.

Summoning the tattered remains of her composure, she went to fetch Arianna, praying the little girl wouldn't sense her agitation. It wouldn't be good for Arianna to pick up on the hostile undercurrents between her governess and parent. Whatever Winnie thought of the insufferable, rude man, a girl needed her papa. Narrowing her eyes to slits, Winnie amended that idea: a girl needed a papa who wouldn't disappoint her. Mr. Dryden hadn't yet failed Arianna. She'd been astonished he'd repainted her room in the green Arianna preferred, but she was glad he'd granted his daughter that indulgence.

Also, it was to the captain's credit that he'd struggled to catch Arianna when she'd flung out of the carriage and that he felt awful he'd failed. It showed the man had a conscience, at least. Given his absence, she'd wondered whether he felt anything at all toward his daughter.

If he failed to come to London so that he wouldn't be forced to court a debutante was it fair to hold his absence against him? That gave her pause.

She was teetering on the point, ready to concede it in his favor when she remembered his stupid suggestion to have Arianna address him as 'sir.' Winnie hardened her heart against the rogue. Didn't he know his daughter chatted about her 'papa' to anyone who cared to listen? Every night in her prayers, Arianna prayed for her papa's hand to get better and for him to teach her how to ride a pony now that he returned from the war.

The tender-hearted girl would be baffled and hurt if forced to call him 'sir.' Mr. Dryden might not prefer to be called 'Papa,' but Winnie was convinced he'd been called worse. Besides, it was easier for him to give on this point than Arianna. Although Winnie didn't wish to challenge Mr. Dryden, Arianna's happiness took precedence.

**

The threesome met in the blue and cream drawing room, which Winnie adored for its serenity. The sum of the room's parts forged something beyond wood, fabric, and plaster for the drawing room had a welcoming air. Mr. Dryden stood by the windows, haloed in deceptive sunshine.

She took a deep breath. "You should be grateful, Mr. Dryden, for Juju and Arianna prayed every night for *her papa's* safe return from the war." She did not look at her employer to see what effect this news might have on him; rather, she glanced at Arianna and told her, "I think you surprised your papa when you threw yourself out of the coach earlier, dear. You must be certain he is ready to catch you before you do such a thing again, poppet."

Arianna's face lost its solemnity and she beamed, first at Winnie then at her father. "I will," she promised. She turned toward Mr. Dryden, her eyes sparkling with mischief, as if to ask, 'Ready?'

Mr. Dryden laughed, squatted, and opened his arms. The pint-size poppet ran across the carpet and hurled at him, flinging her skinny arms around his neck. He stood, hugging Arianna close.

Winnie's throat tightened.

Moments passed before his hoarse voice sounded. "Did you really pray for me every night, Arianna?"

A blonde head bobbed in rapid succession.

Mr. Dryden pressed a tender kiss to the girl's brow. "Thank you."

Winnie sniffed, mortified when Mr. Dryden handed his handkerchief. She accepted it with mumbled thanks.

Mr. Dryden stood, staring at his daughter who clutched a dolly beneath her arm. Miss Lucille was similarly attired in a blue-striped dress and white pinafore. A shadow crept into his eyes, darkening their brown color. Flicking the dolly's chin, he asked, "Is this the dolly Uncle Will gave you? I see her dress matches yours."

This foray into conversational starters for four-year old girls proved the perfect opening gambit. Arianna's blue eyes lit up and she launched into a long tale concerning her prized possession. "This is Miss Lucille, Papa. Uncle Will gave her to me at Christmas, did you know that? He had her made 'pechal just for me, did you know that? He did. We have tea and play together near the fairies pond and she has dresses just like mine. Juju sews them."

Arianna's lips, the color of brightest pink, formed the perfect Cupid's bow; Winnie noted they hardly paused whilst she spoke to her father.

"And I want Juju to sew Miss Monty a dress so we match!" She ended this happy announcement by clapping her hands together, making an emphatic series of nods, as if there could be no disagreement on any of the things she said.

"That's all right and tight then." He smiled and his eyes glowed, yet the shadows lingered. "You will cut quite a dash in society, young lady."

Did she detect a faint hardening in his tone? Winnie frowned, tilting her head toward the man.

As she expected, Arianna returned to Winnie's side, and tucked into the folds of Winnie's skirts. Staring at Miss Lucille, Arianna played with her dolly's hair. Winnie's hand rested on her shoulder, and she gave it a reassuring squeeze. Arianna craned her neck upward and Winnie smiled at her, hoping to remove the sting from her father's voice.

Mr. Dryden stood, cleared his throat, and spoke in a tentative manner, "I brought some gifts for you from Portugal."

"You did?" Arianna squeaked.

Winnie breathed a sigh of relief.

He chuckled. "Of course, I did. Would you care to see them?"

Arianna looked to her for permission, which was conveyed by another pat and nod.

Winnie glanced at Mr. Dryden. She had the sneaking suspicion he'd held his breath while she answered the child's silent question. She frowned. Mr. Dryden might be her nemesis, but he didn't deserve to be snubbed by his daughter. She was dismayed to discover he considered it a possibility. For some reason, his reticence irked her.

"Good." Rubbing his hands together, he spoke with forced brightness. "Shall we go up to my rooms? Spec has unpacked my valise and set the gifts aside."

The girl vacillated. The lure of souvenirs called to her, but her father was still a stranger to her.

Mr. Dryden threw Miss Montgomery a panicked look.

Her lips quirked as she murmured in an under-voice, "Beginning to wonder if you were too hasty selling out your commission?"

His warm chuckle ignited a pleasurable glow within Winnie. She was not sorry for her audacious quip because it removed the bleak, stricken expression from his brown eyes.

Winnie knelt so that she was on level with Arianna. "How delightful to receive new presents! It's a pity we have nothing to give your papa. What were we thinking? Consider, Arianna, how could two intelligent young ladies such as we have been so obtuse?" Winnie smacked her palm against her forehead for good effect, rightfully calculating the girl would be amused by the gesture.

Arianna giggled.

Winnie pressed a finger against her pursed mouth, appearing deep in thought. After a few moments, her eyebrows lifted and she said, "Oh! I have a wonderful idea! Do you know the best gifts my papa wanted from me?"

Eyes as round as an owl's, Arianna asked in awe-struck accents. "No. What?"

Cupping her hand over Arianna's ear, she whispered something into it.

Mr. Dryden remained standing, his carriage erect as always, but he wore a faint expression of amusement on his face.

Arianna giggled then asked, "Really? Really, truly?"

Winnie didn't regret her lie. In truth, Sir Vernon hadn't wanted a single thing from her. "Really, truly."

She cast a sideways glance toward the gentleman. Mr. Dryden watched his daughter with fascination during their silly interlude. He'd answered the call to go to war and for his service, he'd become a stranger to his own offspring. Winnie's heart ached for the patriotic rascal.

"Papa, would you want a kiss as your gift?"

In a flash, Mr. Dryden bent over and presented his cheek. Rather than bestowing a peck there, his daughter flung her arms around his neck, squeezed with all her might, and kissed him full on the mouth.

"Thank you, Arianna," he said after a long bit.

The girl, beaming with delight, then kissed her papa's cheek.

Closing his eyes, he touched the damp spot. "What was that for?"

"Because." She explained in woman's logic, "You're my papa."

Another shadow passed into his eyes before he attempted a brave smile.

His pain struck Winnie.

"Come," Mr. Dryden took Arianna's hand and they walked from the drawing room. "Let's see if you enjoy your gifts."

Trailing behind the pair, Winnie puzzled over her suspicions. She wondered how long he doubted he was Arianna's father. If she were right, she found his assumption of parental responsibility admirable. That thought was as unsettling as toppled ink wells.

Chapter 7

Charles stomped downstairs, his mood already foul. He wore a black jacket tailored by Stultz, satin knee breeches, and an embroidered silk waistcoat in muted gray colors, and a poorly tied cravat. Spec had no experience tying neck cloths and such was patently obvious upon a glance. Even so, it wasn't his appearance that annoyed him so much as it was being late for dinner.

"Ah, there he is, Mama!" Will greeted him as he entered the drawing room.

As he suspected, he was the last to the gathering. He bowed to his mama then to Miss Montgomery, murmuring an apology for being tardy.

His mama came forward and kissed his cheek. Then she stepped back and examined his cravat. "Good Lord, Charles! You didn't have to rush—we would have waited for your valet to tie your neck cloth properly."

"Then you would have waited until the Second Coming of Christ. It took Spec forty minutes and five ruined cloths to achieve this lousy result. He calls it the 'Water Well.'"

Lady Northampton blinked. "I thought the style was named 'Waterfall?'"

"Precisely." Charles turned toward Will. "I'll have a drink, if you don't mind."

"Certainly." Will poured him a glass of red wine, handed it to him as he asked, "How did Arianna enjoy her presents?"

Charles smiled his thanks and drank deeply.

"She adored the lace mantilla," Miss Montgomery answered. "Did you know she wore it all afternoon?"

Will chuckled and patted his concave stomach. "All good and well, I suppose."

"What female doesn't dream of her wedding day?" Charles asked.

Mama preened before the mirror, adjusting her silken turban. Trimmed with an ostrich plume, it was the latest stare in London fashion. Although the countess bemoaned visiting the capital, she always returned with a larger wardrobe. "At this rate, I may attend Arianna's wedding before either of my children's."

"Oh, Mama," Will lamented.

Lady Northampton swatted his arm. "At least Charles has ventured into matrimony, but you, Will! You are the heir and nine-and-thirty. Whatever can you be thinking?"

Charles protested, "Mama!"

"Do not 'mama' me," Lady Northampton shook her head, causing the ostrich feather to quiver with parental disappointment. "If the Earldom passes to one of your father's bacon-brained cousins, the name of Dryden will be as common as…as household lemon polish."

"Mama!" Her sons groaned in unison.

A saucy grin acknowledged her children's embarrassment and that such didn't signify with the countess. She waved toward the dining room. "Shall we proceed?"

"Certainly." Charles polished off the rest of his glass, set it on the side table and extended his arm to the governess.

Miss Montgomery looked at the crook of his elbow as if it were some kind of dangerous weapon. He thought it odd that she was so reluctant to accept his escort for the short stroll to the dining room. Did she believe this show of courtesy exceeded his preference of dispassionate discourse?

He frowned, thinking such a notion was ridiculous, but as he sat the governess, he couldn't fail to detect her stiff back and waves of disapproval which emanated from her. He appeared to be the source of whatever offended her, but he was at a loss what he'd done, other than not having a properly tied cravat. Could the governess possibly be that shallow?

William presided at the head of the table, chatting with his guest and family in a most amenable manner. Lady Northampton sat at the foot, sampling small portions from every dish offered. Charles sat to his brother's right, imbibing at a steady pace while Miss Montgomery's posture grew so rigid, only lumber could emulate it.

In silence, the Canon Ashby servants, renowned for impassivity, served the Dryden family and Miss Montgomery. Bertram, the butler, set bowls of chilled cucumber soup before each diner while holding his breath. In true butler fashion, there were no tics or blinks or jaw clenching to reveal his mindset. Nevertheless, the man made frequent, darting glances in the governess' direction while the footmen served Charles yet another glass of wine.

Miss Montgomery and his mother talked of gathering herbs, which devolved into listing the merits of a particular head cold remedy. Once the women agreed on a recipe, Will volunteered to deliver it to Ol' Nick, the gardener, who suffered from the ailment. Pleased with their tidy disposal of the chore, none realized Charles' temper was unravelling.

"I like whisky," he declared into a conversational void.

No one responded to the bald statement.

Again, he made the attempt to join the table talk. "Whisky is the army's choice for a head cold."

A slight hesitation on his mother's part then she replied, "How interesting."

By sheer dint of will, Charles did not squirm, although his family may well regard him as a candidate for Bedlam.

"Yes, medicinal values found in herbs cannot be over-estimated," Lord Northampton continued after the pregnant pause. "There are a number of books on the subject in the library. Should you wish to avail yourself of them, Miss Montgomery, you are welcome."

"Thank you, my lord." Her lashes raised, those topaz orbs blistering him.

Good God! You would have thought he'd killed a man. All of this because his neck cloth wasn't as it should be? Who was she in her raggedy gown to criticize his attire? Angry at Miss Montgomery's churlishness, he finished his glass of wine and signaled the waiter for another.

Thereafter, his mama made a few attempts to include him, but Charles was stumped, unable to summon a response for small talk. He'd been in the army too damn long where social niceties often went by the wayside. The stream of conversation abated as the others watched him struggle in vain for a *bon mot*. When he had nothing to say the conversation flowed around him in the way the river's current bends around a protruding boulder. His wit could have equaled the boulder this evening.

He downed the contents of his fourth goblet in one swallow.

So he sat at the dining table, aware he should say something, yet unable to do so. His discomfort increased as the meal dragged from one course to the next. Frustration burned his throat. He coated it and retained a tight, resentful grip on his eating utensils to the point of discomfort. Lost in the sulks, he massaged his injured hand.

He sensed Miss Montgomery's gaze resting on his injury. He fumed that his weakness was the sole item which caught her attention. As he glared at her, he saw her large, uneaten portion of meat and his anger drained away. He held his palm out, his fingers beckoning for her plate.

To her credit, she pushed it toward him.

Carving with his left hand, he made a few deft cuts then returned it. "It's difficult to cut meat one-handed, I know." Some mischievous imp prodded him—there could be no sensible explanation—to wink at the governess.

She blushed then murmured her thanks.

A responding inner glow rose inside Charles.

Will mentioned their neighbor, Mr. Peters, was hosting an upcoming house party at Landry House. "I don't care for the low company he keeps. I wouldn't be surprised if it becomes a scandalous gathering. Do not, ladies, I beg of you, enter into any conversations with his guests. I take leave to inform you most are either rogues or rakes."

"It's a pity the squire died without issue." Lady Northampton explained to Miss Montgomery. "Mr. Peters owns a manufactory and purchased Landry House in the last year."

"Yes, once the squire passed, his gamekeeper left. Consequently, vermin have run amuck. I hope Mr. Peters will host a shooting party to rout them from the estate."

During the next course, Charles' contented air dissipated as he ate his bread-encrusted trout with butter sauce. She hadn't smiled at him since he cut her venison. Stymied how to gain her attention, his frustration grew. Charles couldn't recall ever feeling so tongue-tied in a woman's presence. He wasn't a rogue, but he'd charmed his fair share of females. That he couldn't do so with this woman baffled him.

Puzzling over the matter, he consumed his seventh glass of wine. His knife cut across his porcelain plate, creating a 'screeching' sound. Everyone, including the steel-willed Bertram, flinched.

"Beg pardon," Charles murmured into the stunned silence, surprised his speech sounded slurred.

He glanced at the governess. He had startled her. Good, he thought, with no small sense of satisfaction, savoring his trout. He drank deeply from his glass.

Will examined his younger brother more closely. Charles returned his inquiring look with a bland countenance. Will shook his head then directed his attention to their mama's musings regarding interior decor.

"I think dusty rose might suit. Perhaps in silk, Winnie?" Lady Northampton waited for her response.

Miss Montgomery leaned forward, showing greater animation than she had during any point whilst this debacle of a dinner ensued. "Naturally in silk, my lady, but lined to prevent fading. As to the dusty rose? No, rose is not the most flattering color for you."

"Is it not?" Lady Northampton brought her napkin to her mouth and with the other hand, nudged her turban.

Charles' hands hovered over his plate. He broke into the conversation. "Winnie? Is that your given name?"

The governess' gaze slipped toward him, giving him an opportunity to note how startling blue her eyes were. They weren't the kind of watery blue which could be mistaken for grey, but a deep, clear, topaz. As their gazes locked, the color in her cheeks rose and that, too, pleased him.

Considering the matter of her name, Charles nodded in satisfaction as though he'd solved a puzzle. "Short, I suppose, for Winifred?"

"No, Mr. Dryden."

He flexed his good hand, waiting for her to elaborate.

She did not.

They were back at Square One where she refused to give him her name. "Dammit."

Lady Northampton's goblet halted in mid-progression to her lips.

The earl blinked. Twice.

The governess dabbed her napkin to the right edge of her mouth then to the left. Carefully avoiding his quizzing look, she fixed her gaze upon Lady Northampton. "The color rose is most becoming to those of fair complexions, do you not agree, Lady Northampton? With your dark looks, you should choose either gold or crimson."

She thought to ignore him? The reins on his frayed temper began to slip. He closed his eyes to better concentrate on his tenuous hold.

His mother asked, "Crimson? In the breakfast room?"

"It would help one wake up," Winnie urged, a grin in her voice.

Snapping his lids open, he stared at Miss Montgomery. Had he really expected her lovely topaz eyes to greet his? As she gazed at her plate, disappointment washed over him, leaving him dumbfounded and off-kilter.

That slippery grip on the reins of his temper loosened.

He barked, "Only Marshal Ney's advance up the Busaco road was as asinine as you're being, Miss Montgomery!" He referred to the military blunder which delivered the French army into the hands of the combined British and Portuguese forces.

Three mouths dropped, revealing partially chewed food.

"Charles!" The countess squeaked.

"Who are you to sneer at my cravat—" He pulled up short.

A fond mama slapped her utensils against the fine linen tablecloth. "You go beyond the line! Far beyond the line!" Lady Northampton groaned then breached protocol by setting both her elbows on the table. She dropped her head into her hands. Her silk turban teetered for a moment before sliding over her pleated forehead.

"I say, Chas, that's—"

"Stow it, brother." Charles stood. The room whirled around him and he clutched the table, uncertain if his legs would hold him. Dawning dismay replaced his earlier agitation.

Good Lord, I'm drunk. And I've just picked a fight with Miss Montgomery.

The scene took on an unreal, nightmarish quality. His anger turned inward and he brushed the beads of perspiration from his brow, searching for a way to undo the harm he'd caused.

"Charles?" His mother asked.

Winnie Montgomery also stood and placed a fist on her hip. "I am not sneering at your cravat, sir. Excuse me, but I intend to retire now."

"Oh, heavens!" Lady Northampton swished her hand in an ineffectual arc, her headdress askew over a brow.

The butler rushed to her aid, flapping the hem of the tablecloth in his mistress' face to fan her.

"No. You remain. I'll leave, dammit." Charles turned. The tablecloth mysteriously snagged so that as he stepped from the table, everything placed upon it dragged, willy-nilly, in his wake. The crash of dishes breaking and crystal goblets smashing became deafening. Every dish spilled. The contents of a once superior meal erupted from the table, disgorged and tossed like a capsizing ship in turbulent waves. Unable to stay the carnage, two helpless peers, a couple of verbal fencers, and a pair of footmen watched in horror as the wreckage unfolded.

Rebuilding Bertram's stoic reputation might take years. The butler blubbered upon witnessing this culinary catastrophe.

Lady Northampton shrieked and dashed her troublesome turban onto the now-stained carpet.

Will collapsed into his seat, his white palms flashing in mid-air, showing surrender.

Making slow, deliberate moves—for he was reeling from embarrassment—Charles dabbed his napkin at a slather of butter sauce which landed upon his breeches. Into the dead, still silence, he said, "Forgive me for upsetting you all. I apologize for acting like an ass."

No one uttered a syllable, except his mama, who murmured his name on a sigh.

Charles picked up pieces of crockery and set them on the table with soft 'clinks,' which sounded as loud as clashes of thunder in the strained silence.

Bertram appeared to have entered into a catatonic state, unable to move or speak or blink.

"I…I say," William began, his voice faint as he addressed one of the still-aghast footmen, "Could you please procure a basket of sorts? We shall stow the broken pieces in such."

The young man hurried to do his master's bidding, not bothering to hide his relief to escape the hazardous environs.

A teary-eyed Miss Montgomery bit her bottom lip and shook her head in confusion. Hell, he couldn't blame her. His actions tonight mystified him.

She picked up the stained tablecloth by the corners and gathered them with one hand.

"Thank you," Charles murmured, taking the bundle from her. In the process, their hands touched.

"Now is an excellent time for coffee," she said. "Will you join me, Mr. Dryden?"

It was a test. He recognized that much, but did he have a choice?

He nodded.

Lady Northampton addressed the butler. As if his head was fastened to his neck with rusty hinges, Bertram turned toward the countess.

Gathering her dignity, the countess announced, "Dinner's concluded. When you can, please bring some coffee to the drawing room for the family."

Will took his mother's arm and nodded to the two remaining flabbergasted servants. "Thank you. My compliments to Mrs. Halstead."

Chapter 8

A week later found Winnie and her charge dipping their toes into the cool waters of the fairies pond. Giggling as they emptied their shoes of their feet and their feet of their stockings, they splashed one another. Arianna chatted to a small gaggle of geese she'd named Masters, Walford, Maiden, and Lowling. The geese, however, did not appear to share her enthusiasm for conversation and waddled away, their wings unfurling as they squawked.

Winnie laughed at the sight of the four-year old giving chase. She hadn't been this happy in a very long time.

Canon Ashby, an Elizabethan manor, had a box-shaped interior courtyard. Tall, wrought iron gates with ornate pillars flanked the long, pebble drive, promising newcomers a grand estate: it did not fail to deliver upon that promise. The house was made of reddish-brown stones, cut in rectangular shapes laid by meticulous mason workers whose work withstood the challenge of the years. A formal garden extended through a wide, sweeping staircase at the south end of the house. Two urns, spilling with greenery and blossoms, marked its beginning point while a statute of a shepherd boy, so far as to be indiscernible from the house, marked its end. The windows, tall and narrow in the gothic style, contained diamond-shaped panes. Even more formal gardens, influenced by Greek design contained several marble benches from which one could enjoy the topiaries and boxwoods.

Here in the shade of the hawthorn tree Winnie wondered if she hadn't stumbled across Paradise. Like that Biblical garden, though, something sinister slithered in their midst. Winnie had the unsettling notion they were being watched. Several times the hairs

81

raised on the back of her neck until she smoothed them. She scanned her surroundings, but only saw green, rolling hills, a grassy knoll, and thick hedges.

"Oh, Miss Monty! Look!" The girl reached toward a nest, laying on the ground.

"Don't touch it!" Winnie cautioned, scrambling to her feet. She and Arianna knelt beside the starlings' nest and peered inside. Some eggs had broken in their fall, but the winds hadn't been strong enough to dislodge it from its perch. Some naughty neighborhood boy had probably thrown stones at the nest, knocking it from the branches. Did he laugh, the little devil, when it launched from its perch? Was he entertained watching the starlings' home tumble to earth?

She relived the sensation of falling down Stanhope's stairs, as she often did in her nighttime slumbers. Winnie rubbed the phantom pain at the spot where her arm had been broken.

The clopping of nearby hooves sounded. Winnie shoved Arianna behind her, terrified that Sir David would appear, as if summoned by her thoughts.

Charles reined in his gelding, Lightning, and dismounted in a fluid motion. He approached, his voice ringing out, "What's the matter?"

Relief overwhelmed her as she heard the captain's concern. Even wearing a scowl and long hair, his presence reassured her. Something about Mr. Dryden seemed so strong and dependable.

"Papa!" Arianna dashed to her father, hugging his legs.

A smile curved his lips as his hand automatically patted her back. "Arianna!" He echoed the same tone of delight.

She pointed toward the starlings' shattered remains. "We found a nest, Papa. Come look."

Winnie's cheeks flushed as Mr. Dryden caught a glimpse of her bare feet. She mumbled something even she didn't understand as she searched for shoes and stockings. Winnie stuffed her stockings in her sling. Nothing in the world would compel her to don them in Mr. Dryden's presence.

"Mind Lightning," he told his daughter. He led his horse to the pond's edge, tying the reins to a low-hanging branch so the gelding could drink. "What's this about a nest?"

Arianna tugged his hand, dragging him to the place where it came to rest. Standing over the starlings' nest, she inserted her finger into her mouth, garbling, "The babies died."

"That *is* a pity. Leave it be, Arianna, so that the mama will return to her nest and discover their fate." He straightened, looked at his daughter's bare feet and teased, "I see you've been wading in the pond."

Clasping her hands together, the little girl beamed. "Oh, yes, Papa! The water is cool and de—de—what was that word, Miss Monty?"

"Delicious," Winnie supplied, but the fire in her cheeks refused to subside. The innocent word, now spoken in this man's presence, seemed to hint at something naughty.

Winnie sat on the grassy bank, her back toward the father and daughter, fumbling with her shoes, hoping her employer would ignore her immodest show of ankle.

"What was that sound?" Charles asked.

Winnie couldn't dismiss her earlier impression of something havey-cavey, and strained to listen. "Hooves, perhaps?"

Shielding his eyes from the sun, Mr. Dryden said, "Look. Over the crest. There's a rider on a bay. Did you met him?"

"No, nor did he make himself known." She joined Mr. Dryden in a short walk up the hill to watch the departing figures of horse and a man with raven-colored hair.

"Odd."

"Very odd," she agreed, that sickening pit in her belly opening to a yawning gap. She repeated the refrain in her head that Sir David couldn't possibly know her whereabouts, that it wasn't him on the horse, despite the similarity in hair color. All this she told herself, but her hands began to tremble.

Mr. Dryden said, "He's traveling in the direction of Landry House. Must be one of Peters' guests at his house party."

She beckoned Arianna to join her, picking up the girl's shoes and stockings. "Best put on your shoes, poppet. Juju's coming through the garden. We're late for luncheon."

Frowning, Mr. Dryden stooped then brushed her hands aside. "Allow me to do that, Miss Montgomery. Come, Arianna."

He buckled his daughter's shoes then pronounced, "All right and tight."

Winnie ran cold, shaky fingers through her hair. Just thinking of Sir David discombobulated her.

Casting a sidelong glance at her employer, she wondered why he lingered. They had avoided each other for the past week, which seemed the ideal way of dealing with the dinner debacle.

Juju approached, joining them beneath the hawthorn tree. "Good afternoon, Miss Montgomery, Mr. Dryden! Isn't this a lovely morning?"

"It is," Mr. Dryden agreed. "I heard the sounds of giggles and felt compelled to investigate."

"Arianna enjoys the pond," Juju noted with a chuckle.

"And the company of her governess, it seems." Mr. Dryden nodded in her direction.

Winnie's cheeks grew hot again. "Hello, Juju. Arianna and I were just returning."

"I've come to fetch you," she said, her wide smile still in place.

Mr. Dryden caught Winnie's upper arm as she walked passed him and murmured, "A moment of your time, if you will, Miss Montgomery."

Winnie swallowed, dreading whatever scold he would deliver. The heat from his hand soaked through her sleeve and warmed her skin. Before Winnie could decide if the warmth was pleasant or not, though, he released her.

He smiled to Juju in that charming way of his, of which she had caught flashes at Bannock's Inn, but had failed to see since. "Juju, please take Arianna to the nursery while Miss Montgomery and I have a private word."

"Yes, sir." Holding out her hand, Juju waited for Arianna to grasp it.

Walking away, Arianna waved to them over her shoulder, her lips curved in a pink bow. "Goodbye, Miss Monty. Goodbye, Papa."

"Goodbye, poppet." Charles walked up the slope and leaned against the hawthorn tree, his booted heel pressed against the trunk.

Winnie waved goodbye, watching Juju and Arianna's figures become smaller.

She remained at the water's edge, studying the boundary between pond and bank. She fancied she heard the faint echo of Pan's pipe, playing a song for the fairy creatures. The winds moved the long grasses, causing them to sway rhythmically to the satyr's melody. Something about this spot seemed sacred. Here, in Mr. Dryden's company, Winnie felt safe, which was strange given her present worries about the raven-haired rider.

"I apologize for frightening you, Miss Montgomery, when I over-imbibed." His foot left the trunk and he straightened before saying, "In fact, I ask you to forgive all my unkindness. I've acted without cause."

It was such a stark and encompassing admission, she caught her breath. Sir Vernon would never have apologized so grandly.

"Miss Montgomery? Do you forgive me?"

Giving herself a mental shake, she said, "Yes, of course." She hesitated before adding, "And I hope you realize that I wasn't angry that night at dinner because of your appearance—"

"But appalled by my excessive drinking," he said it drily, flinching as he spoke. "Yes. I finally unraveled that mystery with the earl's…ehem…assistance. The coffee helped."

She grinned. "You must be grateful for your older brother's guidance."

"Not entirely, no. Do you have siblings?"

"No."

"Pity."

She gave him a tentative smile.

"You come as a shock to me, Miss Montgomery."

"I do?"

"Yes. When Mama informed me I couldn't discipline you, I was offended. Then to be warned against making improper advances—well, it angered me. After my temper cooled, I began to consider *why* you made such demands."

Winnie stepped backward. Mr. Dryden remained leaning against the trunk. The next few moments passed in silence, and some of her wariness left her. She listened to the wind stirring the grass, certain it was Pan whistling.

"When I came upon the pond, you seemed to be preparing for battle. Did you believe I would attack you?"

"Oh, no…no, sir. You merely startled me, that's all."

The line of his shoulders eased, as if a weight had lifted. Still gazing at her with an intensity she found unnerving, he persisted. "Something concerned you. What was it?"

"N-n-nothing."

Mr. Dryden's giant strides ate up the distance as he rounded Lightning. The gelding tossed his head. He unwound the reins from the branch and let them drop. It was a measure of his confidence in the well-trained horse that Lightning took a few steps before sipping again from the pond. She realized that around his daughter, though, he took the precaution of securing the horse. Winnie suspected Mr. Dryden was becoming a doting father. She smiled.

He came to stand beside her, casting his gaze over the pond. "It's beautiful here, isn't it? It feels other worldly."

Her smile broadened. "I've been imagining fairies communed here. It pleases Arianna."

His head turned toward her, surprise written on his countenance. Chuckling, he said, "I am glad you picked up on the notion. Will and I spent a great deal of time here in our childhood, weaving fantasies." He pointed to another tree whose trunk was gnarled. "We joked the fairies huddled beneath that overhang whenever it rained. It wouldn't do for their wings to become wet."

"Exactly." She beamed, marveling they could reach a perfect understanding. They remained standing, side-by-side, simply watching a fish nip at an insect on the pond's surface.

He flicked the darned cuff of her sleeve. "This won't do."

The brief moment of unity vanished.

"Well, it will have to."

"I had supposed my mother would have seen to it, but you are not outfitted as you should be."

She touched her cheek, embarrassed. "Did you expect me to wear a uniform? I'm sorry I did not—"

"No, I don't expect you to wear a uniform, devil take it!" He frowned so fiercely, Winnie took a backward step.

"Do you mind that this gown isn't made of wool, like my other one?"

"What do I care if it's wool? It isn't the material I object to—it's the fact that this gown is fit for the rag bin."

She blinked before arguing, "Oh, not the rag bin, surely? You see, sir, I had to wear this gown, so that my new one could be washed."

At his horrified expression, Winnie burst out laughing.

"What is it?" He gave a slow smile.

Shaking her head, Winnie explained, "Really, Mr. Dryden, a person only needs one nice gown."

"I disagree, ma'am. Having been married before, I can assure you Vivian's clothespress overflowed with gowns and she still longed for more."

"Well, I can assure you, sir, that thin household budgets don't stretch to cover costs for new gowns. Not when roof repairs are needed."

"Because they're so costly?"

Chuckling, she said, "Yes, but also because one cannot climb onto said roof in a muslin walking dress!"

Her attempt at levity fell flat.

Mr. Dryden's warm, brown gaze rested thoughtfully upon her. His voice was low when he next spoke. "It is my duty as your employer to see you properly outfitted. Allow me to make amends. Tomorrow you must visit the seamstress in Culworth and order new gowns, a warm cloak, and anything else you require. You must also purchase an attractive, new bonnet. My man, Spec, will deliver sufficient funds once we return to the manor."

Winnie's head jerked up and her jaw dropped. "What? Why would you do this?"

He spun from the pond, allowing Winnie to glimpse the frustration on his face. "You must not forget you are a baronet's daughter. That *signifies*. Don't let anyone else forget it, either. You were not born into servitude. Surely your family taught you what is due your name."

"My mother did before she died of influenza."

"How old were you when your mother passed?"

"Fifteen." Winnie's throat tightened. It still hurt to speak of her mama.

Silence reigned. The fish broke the surface again, creating ripples in a futile bid.

Mr. Dryden tilted his head as he considered her, "You know, I do believe I might have met your father, years ago. Playing cards."

She said nothing.

"Ah. You didn't care much for your father?"

She took her time before answering. "Not for his character, no. I suppose I loved him as a little girl, but as I aged I found I couldn't respect him."

"He wasn't honorable?"

"No. The only thing reliable about Sir Vernon was that he put his interests above all else. He gambled away my mother's fortune, my dowry. It was all prescribed in their marriage settlements, but after Mama passed—" She shrugged. "He spent whatever money he could get his hands on, no matter, and no one stopped him."

Mr. Dryden frowned. "The trustees?"

"Useless men."

A dragonfly fluttered about before landing on his shoulder. She whisked it away, murmuring, "Dragonfly."

He watched it disappear, their moods turning contemplative.

"Why do you drink so much, Mr. Dryden?"

It was his turn to hesitate before replying. "I don't know. I've never been a Methodist, but since Busaco...I suppose I, like many other soldiers, drink to forget the horrors of war."

"That's the battle? Busaco? Where you injured your hand?"

"Yes." His voice sounded distant, as if the past had reclaimed him. He caught her hand in an absent-minded gesture. Perhaps he needed to feel a human connection? Winnie held her breath and remained still.

To her embarrassment, he studied the red, roughened knuckles before flipping it over to examine her palm. Very much aware of how her hands betrayed her, for they weren't the hands of a delicate lady of leisure; they were the hands of someone who toiled in the vegetable garden, washed dishes, polished furniture, and chopped firewood.

Mr. Dryden pressed his damaged hand against her good one. "I don't wish to battle you, Miss Montgomery. I am weary of fighting."

Facing her as he did, Winnie should have consumed his field of vision, but she sensed he didn't see her; rather, his gaze leveled on a distant sight.

"You refer to your time in the Peninsula?"

Mr. Dryden said nothing, only dropping her hand to run his palm over the crown of his head. He stooped, picked up a stone, and tossed it between his hands, lost in memories. He flung it into the pond. They watched its ripples.

"Have you ever, Miss Montgomery, shot a man?"

Winnie stammered. "Why, no."

He nodded, expecting this answer. He raised his arm, bent the elbow of the other one, mimicking the action of holding a rifle. "It's accomplished by pulling a trigger with the tip of a finger. Light work, in fact. An explosion propels the ball down the barrel. The rest of the body—the chest, the shoulder, the legs—provides steadiness and bears the brunt of the recoil. By the merest touch, Miss Montgomery, death can be wrought."

Winnie looked at her fore finger, amazed by the whorls on its tip.

He cast another stone into the pond, slinging his arm sideways so that it skipped the pond's surface. "Back to our lessons, Miss Montgomery. I asked if you ever shot a man—easiest thing in the world. Pull a trigger. Now what, do you suppose, is required to stab a man?"

His eyes darkened, the color of darkest night, as he awaited her answer.

She lifted a palm in helpless bafflement, but her companion remained quiet, his gaze fixed upon her. After a while, she stuttered, "I…I suppose there's more physical involvement. Your hand, gripped about a blade's shaft…"

"Or bayonet," he supplied.

She nodded. "Or bayonet."

"Go on."

Winnie closed her eyes, picturing herself in the captain's boots. He'd stabbed a man to death, several, she imagined. She gasped as the image became clearer. "You would have lunged, putting the strength of your…um…body behind the…"

"Very good, Miss Montgomery," he drawled. "Stabbing a fellow requires the use of every muscle in one's body, not just those in one's fingertip. Thereby spreading the guilt throughout one's body." Charles laughed without humor and scratched his nose. "It's not a suitable topic for discussion, especially with a woman. Once more, I must apologize. These black moods overcome my good sense."

Winnie shook off his apology, indicating she hadn't taken any offense. She wasn't a delicate creature with refined sensibilities. She understood the grim side of humanity. She gathered a handful of pebbles then cast them over the water as a farmer would scatter feed amongst the chickens. "It must be much personal. You must feel…"

Charles' head whipped up.

How did he feel?

She recalled how he collected her luggage at Bannock's Inn, even though she'd scolded him. So he was conscientious. When he noticed she couldn't cut her meat, he did so for her, which was thoughtful. His apologies were fulsome, generous. How would such a man feel under attack?

She gave him a considering look, weighing her old impressions of him as a gaming drunkard against this new information. Mr. Dryden, in the heat of battle, must have felt vulnerable, angry, horrified then guilty. Her employer was more complex than she first thought him.

"I will tell you, Miss Montgomery, if you share why you insisted on those conditions of employment."

Shock stilled her tongue and the silence which followed was strained and lengthening.

"Pity," he said eventually. "You may trust me, Miss Montgomery."

Shaking her head to clear her troubled thoughts, she mumbled, "I should return. Is there anything else, sir?"

"No."

"Good day, sir."

"Miss Montgomery?" He stayed her with a light touch on her shoulder.

"Y...yes?"

"I like you better without the blasted spinster's cap. Much more approachable."

Winnie walked to the manor, refusing to look backward. The man by the fairies' pond wasn't the enchanted satyr, Pan; he was just a man. A flawed man, certainly, but perhaps there was more good within Mr. Dryden than she'd given him credit. He was more generous than her father had been, insisting she be properly attired.

She took the stairs to her attic room, a happy bounce in her steps. When she entered her room, she tore the cap from her head and flung it into the corner. Her cheerful mood continued when an hour later, she entered Arianna's room and kissed her awake. With a beaming smile, she said, "Arianna, dear, nap time's finished. We have a lovely day awaiting us."

Chapter 9

The metallic scent of blood crept over him like fog rolling in at dawn. It snaked into his nostrils so that he breathed through his mouth, but even so death left a bitter taste. His legs thrashed, as if he stumbled over blood-slickened bodies. Charles fell, unable to keep his footing. Gore splattered, dousing his coat and drenching his boots. Within his ears the echoes of his slips and curses, the wounded's cries, the dying soldiers' groans sounded. Charles jackknifed in bed, his body awash in sweat.

No matter how many months had passed, he couldn't root out the images from his last battle at Busaco. Charles despaired if he'd ever escape the specter of death. The memories of hand-to-hand combat disturbed him. It helped having Spec around because his former batman shared that experience with him. Neither spoke of their time in Portugal, but they understood each other's nightmares and dealt with them as they came. This morning, however, Spec wasn't there when Charles awakened. He suspected his valet had gone to the tavern the night before for a healthy bout of drinking, swiving, or both. He didn't begrudge Spec his recreation. Lord knows, he wished he had an outlet so he could obtain relief.

Charles pulled on his trousers, shirt, and benjamin coat. Since coming home to Canon Ashby, he'd steered away from spirits, save for that debacle of a dinner. As a recourse to easing his mind, this left a long, hard ride. Morning had already broken as he galloped over the fields. Workers were busy planting crops. He waved to a few, but did not stop to talk with them as he would have done before the war. Lightning sensed his master's mood, taking the hedges without hesitation and flying through the countryside as if demons from hell chased them both. After a few miles, he pulled up, breathing hard. Not wanting to put his horse into a lather, Charles settled into a slow trot and circled around the estate, coming upon the fairies pond.

Squeals of Arianna's laughter greeted his ears and he smiled for the first time that day. He guided Lightning toward the sounds of splashing and giggling. When he came over the rise, he saw the bare-foot governess examining something on the ground with his daughter. Miss Montgomery's hand wrapped about Arianna's waist. The instant she became aware of his presence, Miss Montgomery whirled and shielded Arianna.

Dear Lord, did the governess think she was under attack?

***

From the shade of the hawthorn tree, he watched Miss Montgomery's springy steps take her to the house. What the devil *was* her first name, if not Winifred?

Gratified she didn't view him as a threat, he couldn't dismiss her initial alarm as he approached. She'd been afraid, which led to the next question—who frightened her? Recalling how she'd protected his daughter, he surmised whoever scared the governess was someone she believed was capable of harming a child.

Turning Lightning over to a groomsman, he strode to the house, considering their discussion. What kind of female thought she needed only one decent gown? Who else spoke of repairing roofs in muslin even if joking? He halted. What if she hadn't been teasing? God forbid, what if that woman had actually climbed upon a roof and made repairs?

Sir Vernon might have gambled away her dowry, but surely he hadn't failed Miss Montgomery in other ways. Charles shook his head, continuing his progress to his rooms. The image of those frayed cuffs and that battered basket which contained her belongings passed through his mind, tipping the argument against the baronet and in the daughter's favor. Sir Vernon was a dastard who treated his daughter shabbily.

Had he treated Miss Montgomery any better, though? He'd been openly hostile to her at Bannock's once she refused to give him her name, but it would have been foolhardy for a woman traveling alone to do such a thing. He'd taken offense at her scolding letters. Might he have been overly-defensive there? Mayhap the sharp tone of her correspondence owed more to zeal than shrewish tendencies?

He changed from his riding clothes then left Spec a note to deliver three Sovereigns to the governess for additional wages. Although Miss Montgomery was Vivian's opposite in most characteristics, Charles would never understand either woman. Stripping to his waist, he splashed water on his torso while he considered his marriage. They hadn't celebrated their first anniversary when he discovered his wife with a footman. Vivian's affairs were legion, some lasting only as long as the coupling, others enduring for weeks before she took another lover.

He didn't want to re-live that humiliation, but marry he must.

If he had to be leg-shackled, he might do well to marry the leery governess. She wouldn't be promiscuous. Hell, she hated men.

Chuckling, he lathered his cheeks until they were frothy and after a few passes with the razor's blade, the idea struck him with more force.

What if he married the governess?

He carefully finished shaving, and as he tidied up, several reasons leapt to mind which supported the match. Arianna already adored Miss Montgomery, as did his mother. She loved Arianna, too. It was evident in their exchanges as she listened to the little chatterbox. The governess would make a conscientious wife. Charles rather thought he could be a good husband to her. Bedding Miss Montgomery wouldn't be a problem—in fact, he imagined begetting children with her could be enthusiastic.

What the devil *was* her Christian name?

When he stood in the drawing room, Charles searched for traces of him in Vivian's child and found none. Then Arianna kissed him, called him 'Papa,' and those doubts ceased to matter.

He was Arianna's Papa.

Although Miss Montgomery defied him, he wouldn't quibble with her results. She was intelligent, kind. Her laughable efforts to hide her feet bespoke a becoming amount of modesty. He grinned, recalling those shapely ankles. He had some good, raw material with which to work. Yes, he decided, Miss Montgomery could very well be a decent wife for him. The possibility was worth exploring.

He examined two small nicks he'd made while shaving, pleased with his progress. He used the strop belt to sharpen the razor before stowing it away.

"Ah! You're finally here, I see." Spec entered his chambers from the dressing room and put some freshly laundered shirts into his armoire. "Quite a morning, eh?"

Charles chuckled as he approached the clothespress. "I believe you enjoyed yourself better last night than I."

Spec grinned as he lay out the clothes for his employer to wear. "Aye, captain. The wench called Sally was the very *pineapple* of friendliness."

Pausing in the midst of donning his britches, Charles squinted, trying to decipher his valet's meaning. "*Pineapple?*"

The valet rolled his eyes and explained to his slow-witted employer. "The very *epic tome* of friendliness."

Trying to keep from grinning, Charles clarified, "You spent the evening with Sally, who proved to be the *pinnacle* and *epitome* of friendliness."

Spec tugged on his shirt cuffs. "Aye, captain."

"Damned if I don't buy a dictionary for you yet, Dogberry."

His valet handed him a clean cloth then motioned for him to wipe his cheek.

Charles did, afterward glaring at the red-stained cloth. "Damn the French."

"Most gentlemen have their valets shave them. Why you insist on doing it yourself..." Spec handed Charles his linen shirt.

He pulled the shirt over his head, muffling his curses.

"Has Arianna already had her luncheon? I thought to take her to the clearing for a picnic."

"She's not here. Miss Montgomery, Lady Northampton, and Arianna just left to call upon the tenants."

Deflated, Charles wandered downstairs for luncheon. Afterward, he sought out Will's company. They spent the next hours in Northampton's study, discussing estate matters, crop prices, and prospects for harvest.

"How did you find Kedington?" William asked, referring to Charles' estate near Sheffield.

"Fine, although some minor repairs are needed and the drive needs to be re-graveled. Spec hired a cook, Mrs. Huggins. Her husband is the factotum. From what I observed, poor Mr. Huggins does whatever else his wife directs."

Lord Northampton chuckled. "Sounds like an ideal marriage."

"For the wife, undoubtedly it is." Charles' eyes twinkled. "Once we take up residence, I'll hire more staff."

"Ah, yes! And pray, darling brother, when might that be?"

Charles lifted an eyebrow and Will laughed, raising his palm. "I didn't mean that the way it sounded. At least, Arianna's welcome to stay at Canon Ashby forever. It's *your* ugly mug I'll not miss."

"Thank you, Will," he said. "For that bit, I'll lengthen my original stay to twice as long."

Both brothers chuckled, but when the laughter died down, Charles said, "I wish to stay a while, if that pleases you. I want Arianna to become accustomed to my presence before spiriting her away from the only home she's known. I still don't know if Mama wishes to join us at Kedington or not."

Will shrugged. "Mama will do as it pleases her."

"Doesn't she always? I instructed Mr. Huggins to send my correspondence here."

"And are you capable of answering your correspondence?"

Charles did not care for the skepticism he read on his brother's face. He expelled a breath of air in gusty frustration. "Writing left-handed is a damnable chore, I don't mind telling you. I struggle with it, but I'm determined to adapt."

"Perhaps you should hire a secretary?" Will scratched the side of his nose.

"No." Charles stood, signaling the end to this unwelcomed conversation. "I won't relinquish my business duties to someone else."

"Not even if your handwriting is illegible? I grant you, it's always been deplorable, but…"

"It'll improve," Charles insisted, his good hand bunching into a fist.

"I hope your shaving improves, as well, before your cheeks are nicked to shreds," Will said with a sharpness Charles was unaccustomed to hearing from his older brother.

Taken aback, Charles shifted his weight onto the other foot and demanded, "What gives?"

No trace of humor appeared in Will's eyes now. He rapped his knuckles on the desktop and barked, "Does it ever occur to you, Charles, that you might need some bleeding help? Has the notion never crossed your mind that your family welcomes the opportunity to assist you? That we wish to support you because we *love* you? You needn't do everything alone!"

"Bloody hell!" Charles sat heavily on the chair he'd just vacated. Resting both elbows on his knees, he dashed his hands through his hair. "Bloody hell," he said, quieter this time.

Raising his brow to new heights, Will waited a beat then drawled, "Let me hire a secretary for you. I can place a post in *The Times.*"

Slumped in the chair, Charles felt as if he'd been leveled with a blow. He waved off the suggestion.

"Chas, this is ridic—"

Charles raised his hand to forestall Will's protest and spoke his next words in a much calmer voice. "I heard what you said. It never occurred to me you might wish…" He cleared his throat, seeing the quagmire he created for himself, but trailed off and shrugged. "I wasn't rejecting you. It's just…"

"Why won't you let me inquire for a secretary?"

"I have someone else in mind for the position," Charles slapped his knees as he rose from the chair. "Someone I already employ."

Will's head shook in mock regret. "Lord, can Spec even spell? Don't tell me you're going to dictate your letters to him!"

97

Charles threw his head back and laughed. "No, I'm not thinking of Spec. I employ another, remember?"

Bemusement crossed Lord Northampton's face. Wrinkling his brow, he searched for the answer and eventually gave up. "Who, then?"

"The governess, Miss Montgomery."

"Icicle? Are you mad, venturing into arctic terrain?"

"Careful, darling brother."

***

At odd times during the afternoon Charles wondered about Miss Montgomery, but didn't have a chance for a *tête-à-tête*. When the three females of the household returned for afternoon tea, they were accompanied by the vicar, Mr. Henry Turnbull, and his sister, Miss Agatha Turnbull.

Henry Turnbull was not a man whose form was pleasing. Along his flushed cheeks, his face had creases which were not, upon closer inspection, wrinkles or the marks of laughter; rather, his habits for gluttony were so pronounced the fleshy parts of his face became puffy. Rotund in the belly, thighs, and ankles, the man could not, with any showing of grace, fold a leg over the other. His walk resembled a duck's waddle, but what annoyed Charles was Mr. Turnbull's air of priggish superiority. In addition to that flaw, Charles found the vicar's flattery of his mother to be nothing less than toad-eating.

"Ah, Lady Northampton!" Vicar Turnbull gushed after lowering himself into the sturdiest chair in the drawing room. "How wonderful it is to see you blessed with the presence of your dutiful sons—is that creamed cake? Oh, I say, how splendid for you to have remembered my favorite. You are the most esteemed among the parish! Such an honor to sit in your exalted presence and to partake of your refreshments as nectar from the gods."

His mother said nothing but prepared the vicar's tea without inquiring to his preference. That the gentleman was so frequent a visitor his mother knew how he took his tea annoyed Charles. As the good reverend's ability to communicate suspended while he consumed the cakes, Charles devoted his attention to Miss Turnbull, the vicar's sister. His brother introduced them and reminded Charles that Miss Turnbull concocted herbal remedies. Perhaps she could suggest an ointment for his hand?

Agatha Turnbull was a spinster who'd never learned the art of flirtation. As her brother's opposite, Agatha Turnbull had a near-skeletal look, which was as displeasing as the reverend's obesity. Miss Turnbull appeared to be all elbows and angles. Her height surpassed her brother's, earning her the sobriquet of "long Meg." Moderation, Charles mused, was not inbred into this pair of siblings.

He doubted whether either Turnbull would recognize the portrait they presented to the world of one who did too much and one who did too little. The spinster sister must have once dreamed of having a family of her own, yet from her discussion Charles surmised she lavished her maternal propensities upon her brother's parishioners.

"May I, Mr. Dryden?" She took Charles' hand into her own and inspected both sides in a detached, clinical manner. "Bayonet?"

"Yes," he acknowledged, self-conscious.

She nodded, pleased with her assessment. "The muscles are tight, inhibiting movement. I would recommend a specially prepared salve made with cayenne pepper. The heat will help loosen those fibers. You will have to massage it into your hand six times a day."

"So often?"

"Yes, sir, if you wish to regain the use of your hand."

"This is plain talking, indeed."

Charles risked a sidelong glance toward his brother, but didn't capture Will's attention. Miss Montgomery took pains to avoid his gaze; how he received the impression she was on the verge of giggling, he didn't know, but there it was.

Before the Turnbulls departed, his mother extended dinner invitations for that evening, which Charles viewed with chagrin.

Miss Montgomery returned to her duties following tea, thereby hindering his ability to draw her into private conversation. Walking upstairs, his foot hovered above a step as he remembered he also needed to inform Miss Montgomery she would be performing secretarial duties for him. This would allow him greater opportunity to convince her he wasn't a gambler, womanizer, or drunkard. He was reliable, unlike her father. If he were going to court Miss Montgomery, he needed to lay a solid foundation and overcome her mistrust. With this strategy, he rubbed his hands together and marched to the nursery.

***

"I won't do it."

Charles blinked. "What do you mean you won't do it?"

Miss Montgomery repeated in that prudish voice, "I won't be your secretary."

"You'll receive additional compensation. Is that the problem?" He tried to erase the scowl from his features, but didn't succeed.

"No, that's not the problem. You can't just march up the stairs, and order me to become your secretary."

That took him aback for that's precisely what he did expect. Did she not realize the natural order of matters? He was the boss, used to issuing orders. She, as his employee, should accustom herself to following them.

Charles inhaled sharply, gaining sudden insight. There wasn't anything remotely docile about Winsome Montgomery. Why had he assumed otherwise? She had challenged him from the first moments of their acquaintance. Part-irritated and part-charmed, she nevertheless fascinated him to a degree no other woman had.

She withstood his exasperation, tucking a loose strand beneath that hideous spinster cap.

Pointing at the offensive headgear, he observed, "I thought you weren't going to wear that blasted thing anymore."

Without batting an eye, she replied in that cool tone he was learning to hate, "Arianna, please disregard your father's unseemly language."

"Beg pardon," he said, bowing to his daughter, his nanny, and the governess. "Juju, would you please supervise Arianna while Miss Montgomery and I have another word?"

Without waiting for Juju's reply, Charles' hand clamped onto Miss Montgomery's elbow and he guided her to the corridor in a determined walk. He shut the door with a snap, leaned against it then glared at the uncooperative spinster.

She reminded him, "You once indicated the amount you pay me is excessive, so I fail to see why you'd pay me additional sums—I mean, additional to the money I received this afternoon from Spec. Thank you, by the way."

"Your stubbornness is only half as annoying as your ability to recall my misstatements, word for word." His mouth twitched in humor and when he saw it reflected on her face, he knew a relief out of proportion to the act. "My dear Miss Mont—"

"I am *not* your dear Miss Montgomery."

He grimaced at his mistake. "Beg pardon. You're right to remind me. Miss Montgomery, will you please write some letters on my behalf? With my hand so damaged, it's difficult to answer correspondence."

Referencing his injury was a low, mean ploy, designed to play upon the lady's sympathies, but he did so without compunction. Charles wanted to spend time with Miss Montgomery to prove he wasn't the dissolute rogue she imagined. He wanted her to admire him as much as he esteemed her.

She gave him one of her sparrow looks, tilting her head. Afraid he'd make a mull of matters again, he kept his expression blank. She must have reached a decision, for all at once, she grinned. Her brilliant smile arrowed straight to his chest.

"I'll do it on two conditions."

"God preserve me," he muttered, bracing for the worse. "Well? What are they?"

She *tsked*. "Don't be so chicken-hearted."

His brows spiked. "I assure you, ma'am, I'm no such thing."

"Of course," she said in a placating tone, which he could have resented if she hadn't touched his forearm.

It was the first time she'd touched him. He didn't know if she was aware of the significance of that gesture, but by the saints in heaven, he sure did. Miss Montgomery liked him. He tried not to smile.

"Name your conditions."

"Five pounds annum? I'll credit the amounts paid today against it."

"Done." He smiled, thinking her a paltry mercenary. "And the second?"

"Trim your hair."

"What?" He jerked away from the door. "No! Absolutely not."

"Why not?"

"You've no right to ask such a thing! Do I remark on your appearance?"

She arched a skeptical brow.

He ran his finger beneath his poorly-tied neck cloth. "Look, it's not the same thing. The last man who approached me with a blade did this." He raised his injured hand.

"So that's why you shave yourself and refuse to be barbered? You can't trust someone to do those things for you?"

Filled with anger, he regretted his desire to improve their acquaintanceship and railed at himself for entertaining the stupid idea that he might marry her.

Again, she touched his forearm. Her words and eyes were soft as she apologized, "I didn't understand. Now I do and I'm very sorry. Forget the second condition."

She'd left him uncertain whether he could claim a victory here or not, the little minx. Gathering his composure, he announced, "We can begin tomorrow at luncheon, if that's acceptable?"

"Fine. Juju can give Arianna her meal and then oversee her nap while we work."

"Excellent." Charles clapped his hands then paused, his eyes narrowing. "Er…what *is* your Christian name, ma'am?"

"Winsome."

His heart skidded against his ribcage for no apparent reason. He took his time answering, but his voice was wry when he did. "No wonder you rate your attractions so high."

She chuckled as he opened the door then motioned her through the portal.

As he walked downstairs, he smiled at the rich sounds of Winsome Montgomery's laughter.

Chapter 10

Miss Montgomery was, in Charles' estimation, the most obstinate, yet entertaining, female he'd ever met. Throughout the afternoon, he'd worked in his study with the window open. Female chatter and the occasional giggle drifted in as he poured over his papers—the delightful sounds soothed him and restored his belief that the world was not yet lost.

"Why are squirrels called squirrels?" He heard Arianna ask her governess.

"Because their tails are so bushy," Winsome Montgomery replied. "And see at the end, how it swirls? Well, obviously, somebody must have once called them 'Swirls,' but through the years, the name changed to 'Squirrels.'"

Silently he approached the window to watch the pair. He could never play cards with the governess—her face was too expressive; however, observing the animation within her countenance pleased him as few things did. The notion of marrying her had already lost its foreign feel. If he must produce an heir for the earldom, he could do much worse. Winsome—as he'd begun to think of her—was intelligent, kind, and amused him. She had the unfortunate habit of knocking him off-balance, emotionally speaking, but he reckoned life with her wouldn't be boring.

Later as he prepared for bed, Charles asked Spec, "Have you made any progress on discovering why Miss Montgomery entered service?"

"No, captain, but she appears to be alone in the world, save for a second cousin, Sir David Broomstead, who inherited the baronetcy. Sir Vernon died in the Fleet in early February. Sir David and his wife, Gwendolyn, came to Stanhope shortly before Miss Montgomery arrived on the earl's doorstep."

Arrested in the middle of removing his shirt, Charles demanded, "The new heir put out his dependent?"

"From what I gather, Sir David appears to be entirely insubbortable."

His mind on heftier matters, Charles corrected Spec, "It's a 'p', not a 'b.' You're thinking of insubordi*nate.*"

"Just what I said." The valet *tsked,* shaking out the discarded shirt and breeches before draping them over his forearm.

Charles extended his hand, silently asking Spec to hand him his robe. "I must marry."

"Captain?"

"Yes, dammit. Marry."

"But I thought you didn't like being married," Spec said.

"I didn't. The lay of the land, however, is thus: I must provide an heir for the earldom. To do that, I need a wife. My first wife, Vivian, whom you fortunately never met, had the heart of a trollop. So, since I must marry, I'm determined to find a faithful wife." He eyed his valet before saying, "What do you think of Miss Montgomery as a candidate for marriage?"

"Miss Monty?"

Charles nodded.

"The governess?" Spec asked, seeking clarification. "The one who dislikes you?"

With an annoyed jerk of his head, he said, "Stop the theatrics. You know damned well I've grown on her."

Spec chuckled. "Aye, Captain. I watch her with Arianna. It's clear she loves the little girl."

"And?"

"She's wary," Spec said, rubbing his chin. "But I think perhaps she's warming up to you a bit."

"I agree."

"If you wish to court Miss Montgomery, you should know she's in the habit of taking an early morning walk through the south gardens. Anything else, Captain?"

"Thank you, Spec. Wake me in time that I may join her tomorrow, won't you? Goodnight."

"Goodnight."

Morpheus, however, chose to send his own thief to steal Charles Dryden' slumber. Haunted by bloody images—this time placing Winsome Montgomery in the heat of the battle, Charles tossed and turned. Giving up on sleep, he threw off the covers with a violent curse and donned his dressing robe. Walking downstairs with a brace of candles, he berated Spec for not leaving a decanter of brandy in his rooms. From the corner of his eye he saw a shadow move on the back stairwell. Alert, he followed it on padded feet.

A dark, slender form, clad in a billowy mass of material made its way toward the kitchen. Holding a candlestick aloft, she moved slowly. He recognized that incongruence for his dear Miss Montgomery, and decided a detour was in order.

"Not able to sleep, eh?"

"Oh!" She whirled, fists clenched, her hair swinging about her face. "Why must you always startle me?"

Her hair was platinum, glistening beneath the candlelight like a firmament of heavenly stars. In his nine-and-twenty years, Charles Dryden had never seen a woman's hair half as lovely as Winnie Montgomery's. He recalled he'd thought it a lovely shade at the fairies pond, but the shade had dimmed its beauty. Belatedly, he became aware he'd been staring like a moon-calf. He sought to recover lost ground by employing a sense of humor. "It's not my fault you're as edgy as a mouse kept in close quarters with an owl, a hawk, and a cat."

Her hand rested on her hip as she gaped at him. Bemused, she repeated his words. "As a what near an owl?"

"As a mouse near a hawk and a cat," he finished for her, smiling as he did so.

Miss Montgomery, in her finest governess demeanor, drew herself up to her full, unimpressive height and spoke in reproving tones, "I've never heard of such a thing."

He made a self-effacing gesture, trying to assume the mantle of modesty, but failed when his triumphant smile broke free.

She hadn't missed it and responded with sarcasm, "Why, how very droll you are, to be sure."

Charles chuckled. "Listen, I intended to sneak downstairs for some brandy, but if you ask me nicely, I'll join you for a cup of warm milk instead."

"You shouldn't drink, you know."

"I've no intention of becoming a teetotaler, Miss Montgomery."

She frowned. "No, I wouldn't wish that. You've already said you were no Methodist."

"But you don't approve of my drinking."

"I don't approve of over-indulging."

"I'm working on it. Share some warm milk with me and ensure my sobriety."

She glanced at the door, hesitating, but he led her to the kitchen.

"Come, Miss Montgomery. I, too, am unable to sleep. No reason we can't double the recipe."

He brushed by her, enjoying the heat of her body. The temperature of his own rose a few notches in response. Without making a production of his perusal, he skimmed her form and lamented the opaqueness of her flannel robe.

"You'll warm the milk, Mr. Dryden?"

With false bravado, he replied, "I served in the infantry. Watch and observe, Miss Montgomery, a true military hero in action. You might learn something."

Grinning, she urged him, "By all means, then, don't allow me to distract you from such daring feats. Although, I should warn you that if you break any of Cook's crockery, she'll flay you alive, hero or not."

"Duly noted." He clicked his heels together and eyed her narrowly. "No doubt you'd be the first to carry the tale to her."

Looking younger than her admitted age, a devilish gleam entered Miss Montgomery's eyes as she *tsked*. "I've never been a tattler, although..." she allowed her voice to trail off. "In your case, I might make an exception."

"Minx," he murmured. He lifted the brass curfew from the banked fire, delighted to find he only needed to add some wood to

106

stoke it higher. He opened a few cabinets before he turned to asked, "Don't suppose you know where the cook keeps the half-kettle?"

"Asking for reinforcements so soon?" A slender eyebrow arched.

He enjoyed the teasing banter. Yes, Miss Montgomery was a worthy opponent. They might just rub along nicely in a marriage.

"No, no. It's a matter of testing your knowledge, nothing more."

She bit her bottom lip but pointed to the half-kettle kept on the fire back for warming water.

He muttered something as he reached for it.

Miss Montgomery shook her head in mock despair.

Charles wandered into the pantry, viewing the well-laden shelves. Popping his head out the door frame, he queried, "Um…where can the milk be found?"

Without speaking, Miss Montgomery indicated the icebox in the cellar.

"Aha!" Charles uncovered the pitcher of milk.

"At this rate, I may yet fall asleep," his companion observed. "I like my milk with honey and cinnamon. Do you?"

He scratched his head. "I've never tried it before. Juju used to make Will and me hot toddies with whisky, honey, and peppermint. I imagine it's close to the same." He placed some oak on the kitchen fire and used the bellows to bring it to life.

"Hardly," she said.

It was his turn to *tsk*. "Careful now, Miss Montgomery. That could be construed as criticism and you don't wish to sound churlish."

"No, no," She hastened to correct him—glancing at his face, though, she realized he'd been teasing her. "I'll fetch the honey and cinnamon, shall I?"

"You really do admire her, don't you? Juju, I mean." Charles poured milk into the half-kettle, set it on the pot hook then swung the crane arm over the fire.

"Oh yes, I like everyone here. Canon Ashby's been very good for me."

"Would you please set out some cups? I'll shave the cinnamon."

"Oh, leave that. Use the stick to stir it."

"What?"

She giggled at his dismay. "Oh, for heaven's sakes!"

He smiled, gratified she had, at long last, lowered her guard.

Attuned to his male appreciation, her grin slipped off her face and her countenance cooled.

He damned the setback; he hoped her walls would have stayed down longer. Charles was baffled what to do with the return of the chilly frost. He scowled into the depths of the half-kettle then poured the milk into the cups.

Winnie wiped up a tiny spill he'd made.

"Thank you."

"Not at all," she said.

Theirs was a commonplace conversation, but its ordinariness reinforced his notion they worked well as a team.

Charles leaned back, stirred the honey into his milk with the cinnamon stick and took a tentative sip. "Hmmm," he said after the first sip.

Winnie drank. He waited with a cocked eyebrow.

"Better than brandy," she decreed, smiling her reassurance.

"Doing it much too brown, Miss Montgomery."

That brought a soft smile to her flushed countenance, a circumstance which gratified him. Silence descended upon the pair as they enjoyed the cozy kitchen and the quietude. The household was asleep. Light beams cast from a lantern illuminated their space, flickering and teasing, causing Charles' knots of tension to unfurl. His companion, also seemed relaxed. Together they watched the fireplace's glowing embers dance and throb.

"Juju's birthday is next month," Charles mentioned it because his old nurse was very much on his mind of late. She tired more quickly now, unlike her old self. Before the governess could reply to that observation, he asked, "You plan to go the dressmaker's tomorrow?"

"Oh yes! I shall order two dresses, a cloak, and a new bonnet. You…you haven't changed your mind, have you? I mean, about me not wearing a mob cap?"

He assured her, "I never change my mind."

"Yes," she nodded. "I've noticed you're quite stubborn."

This observation, cloaked in layers of insulating, blinding righteousness, caused Charles to choke.

Tilting her head, she gave him her familiar 'sparrow' look. "Lady Northampton wishes to order a new dress and a petticoat for Arianna."

"Fine. Have you decided on any colors?"

"For Arianna?"

"No, not for Arianna. For you."

She screwed her nose up as she said, "Navy and brown would be most practical…"

Charles shuddered. "Not for your coloring. The brown will wash you out completely!"

She looked taken aback. "What would a soldier know of flattering colors?"

"A damned sight more than you, apparently."

Shaking her head, she scolded, "There's no need to swear."

"And don't get something that buttons all the way to the neck, devil it."

"You just swore again."

He grinned his unrepentance then promised himself he'd improve her wardrobe later. He wasn't about to let her purchase new, ugly dresses to replace old, ugly ones.

"May I accompany you to the seamstress' shop tomorrow? I'd like to purchase a birthday gift for Juju." Which was true, but not absolutely true. He'd speak to the dressmaker and countermand her orders. "Do you think Juju would be pleased with a shawl?"

"I think that's very kind."

"Well, I believe she's going to turn sixty, so it's a milestone."

The governess slapped the table. "Fifty-seven! Why can't military heroes correctly guess a lady's age?"

He laughed outright, jostling his cup, and spilling milk onto his robe.

She handed him the dish towel she'd used and continued her scold, "For heaven's sake, if you must take a guess, then lower the number by a decade!"

"And if I do know the accurate number, I should suggest the lower number, anyway?"

She grinned. "Well, it certainly wouldn't hurt…"

Companionable silence fell upon them once again. Charles searched his brain for some conversational gambit, but Miss Montgomery came to the rescue by commenting, "Arianna would have loved this." She motioned to her half-full cup.

"Yes. You were right." He folded his hands on top of one another, resting them on the scarred surface of the kitchen table.

She gave him a dry look and said, "Of course. What about specifically?"

"About Arianna being so bright and sweet-natured."

The warm, affectionate light entered her eyes when his daughter's name was mentioned. Winsome gazed at the fireplace then swiveled her head to stare at his clasped hands resting on the tabletop. A strange intensity entered her expression and Charles squirmed, not at all sure what he'd said or done to merit this heightened attention.

She smiled, folded her own hands then nodded for him to take note. "Do you see the difference in how our hands are held?"

"No."

"Look again. Look closely," she urged.

He studied his hands then hers. Nothing significant struck him until he observed the dominant side. "Are you left-handed?"

Vigorously, she shook her head. Her eyes sparkled as she denied it. "I'm not."

Puzzled by the excitement which made her squirm in her chair, he studied the two sets of folded hands and tried to discern her meaning.

"Most people hold their hands like this—" She demonstrated the left thumb resting atop the right thumb. "You do it the opposite way—your right thumb's on top. That's rare. It has nothing to do with being right-handed or left-handed."

110

"And the significance is?"

Leaning toward him, she whispered, "Arianna holds her hands the same way, too."

Now she'd captured his attention. He stared into her shining, topaz eyes, wondering whether she knew his doubts about Arianna's paternity.

She made a sly smile.

She knew!

Nonchalantly, she commented, "It's something to think about, at least."

Charles had no words to fill the silence that followed. His initial reaction had been anger, but that flame burned out quickly. Miss Montgomery, without attempting to embarrass either him or his daughter, sought to reassure him of his rightful parentage. It was generous of her and he appreciated her for it.

Tonight, perhaps, he could begin returning the favor. His voice low, he asked, "Why can't you sleep?"

"It's of no consequence." She shoved her cup away.

"I wouldn't have asked if it weren't important."

Charles could have sworn the woman shrank into her kitchen chair. Before the silence became unbearable, he changed the topic. "Do you know what else is worth thinking about?"

"No. What?"

"Forts," he enunciated.

"Forts?" She frowned, thrown off by the *non-sequitur*.

He nodded, walking to the fireplace to fetch the kettle of warmed milk. He lifted it, offering more. She pointed to her cup, answering him by deed. He poured, replenishing both drinks. "Forts are designed for protection. The best ones have high, strong walls. Don't you agree?"

"I suppose." The admission pulled from her.

"But inside a fort is a very dim place. No sunlight gets through the outer walls." He returned to his chair and sipped his honeyed milk. "The problem with having walls, Miss Montgomery, is that one misses sunshine."

Her eyes darkened with worry as her face paled.

"Living in a world without sunshine isn't living well, is it? Not really."

The young lady stared at the table, tracing a scar in its surface. Then she folded a pleat into the lap of her flannel robe. After the first was finished, she did another then another. She had a row of anxious pleats before she found her tongue.

"Forts are safe places, though, Mr. Dryden."

"You are safe at Canon Ashby."

Her lashes flickered up to watch him as he spoke. She gathered the lapels of her robe, a defensive gesture which stung his heart. Then she rose so quickly from her chair, her thigh rammed the table leg.

Charles winced in sympathy. "Are you well, Miss Montgomery?"

"Thank you for the warm milk, sir. I shall see myself to bed. Goodnight, sir."

He remained seated, struggling with the impulse to fetch her back so he could kiss her. The whim wasn't born from lust; rather, it was born from the wish to lend her some of his strength because he believed she needed it. Odd that the silver-haired icicle aroused his protective instincts.

Instead, he murmured, "Goodnight."

"And…thank you for the…milk." Her slippered feet whisked against the planked floor as she scurried across the kitchen's sanded hearth.

Sighing, he set the kitchen to rights, banking the fire, covering it with the curfew again, and putting back the screen before returning to his bedchambers. Something troubled her, yet she refused to confide in him. Stubborn girl. What would it take for her to trust him?

Beneath the cool façade hid Winnie Montgomery's true self and he'd caught a glimmer of it tonight. Warm, generous, amusing. At her core lay a diamond with brilliant fire, which she concealed for so long, even she seemed to have forgotten the treasure she carried within her.

Climbing the staircase, his earlier hunch that Winnie would make him a suitable wife was confirmed. He marveled how comfortable and tranquil he'd felt during the cozy chat. He never felt so with Vivian. Even as children, Vivian had been annoying. He recalled her coming across him while he was fishing. Despite his repeated requests for quiet, she giggled and chattered, driving not only the fish away, but his desire to be outdoors, as well.

He rather thought he could spend a whole day lazing about the river's bank, fishing with Winnie. Most women wouldn't consider that a high compliment, but to Charles it seemed ideal. Inwardly, he pictured a summer's day in the hopefully, not-too-distant future: he'd bait the hooks while she reeled in fish. There would be laughter and joy in those outings he was certain. Could he achieve the kind of contentment with Winsome that his first marriage had lacked?

She was a restful woman, true, but he also enjoyed rousing her ire. He removed his robe and grinned. My, how her topaz eyes could flash in annoyance and sparkle in delight.

His last thoughts before he fell asleep were who frightened Winsome? What caused the shadows in those lovely eyes?

Chapter 11

"Quick! Carry it away, Flynn. Miss Montgomery, a moment, please!" Charles Dryden snapped his fingers at the Scottish groom then signaled her to stay put.

Winnie halted.

Flynn, the surly Scottish stable hand, bent over what appeared to be the mounting block. Jeb, the head groom, obstructed her view. Mr. Dryden shuffled next to him, lending his bulk so that she could not peer around the pair to see what Flynn was doing. He lugged the mounting block around the stables, his broad back concealing his precise activity. When Flynn was out of sight, Mr. Dryden beckoned her forward.

"Forgive us, Miss Montgomery. I've been chatting with Jeb."

"Yes, I heard the commotion and came to inquire."

"Oh, yes, well…" Mr. Dryden blushed.

Winnie's steps slowed as she noted the strained atmosphere. Her gaze traveled to Rupert, the stable lad of twelve years. His eyes were red-rimmed and he sniffed, wiping his nose on his sleeve. "Rupert? Are you all right?"

"Y…yes, Miss Monty." Unable to keep his composure, Rupert dashed to a stable stall, gulping for air.

Astounded, she turned a questioning gaze toward Mr. Dryden. "What's upset Rupert? Has he been hurt?"

"No." Mr. Dryden's lips tightened.

"Have you angered Jeb, Rupert—" She flung her hand toward the side of the building. "Flynn, as well?"

114

"Me? Me?" Mr. Dryden's thumbed pressed against his chest.

"Yes, you," she snapped. "Everyone's acting stran—"

"Well, I like that! Immediately, you think the fault lies with me!" Mr. Dryden puffed out his chest, but his indignation struck a false note with Winnie. He glanced sideways, leaving her with the impression he searched for Flynn's return.

She asked in far gentler tones, "What is it? What's wrong?"

"We shall not discuss it."

"Why not?"

"Not now, Winsome."

She noticed his gentle rebuke and his use of her Christian name. Winnie nodded, accepting the questions would have to wait to be answered.

Jeb exited the stables, leading Lightning. He nodded to Winnie and murmured, "Good morning, Miss Montgomery."

She stared at Jeb in his wide-brimmed, felt hat. He fidgeting, refusing to meet her gaze. A feeling of unease drifted over her and Winnie felt out of sorts. The groomsmen behaved with unnatural awkwardness, making her chary. Every morning since coming to Canon Ashby, she stopped at the stables, fed sugar cubes or apples to the horses, and patted their long noses, cooing to each as she did so. Winnie derived great pleasure in being, once again, amongst fine horseflesh. She'd missed the smells and sounds of a bustling stable.

Mr. Dryden's presence was the only thing unusual about this morning; he must have done something to set the stable hands on tender hooks. She shook her head, confused by that conclusion. How could he have offended stable hands, men not normally known for having delicate sensibilities? Would Mr. Dryden make a child cry? Neither scenario seemed likely. Mr. Dryden was proving to be an affectionate father, unlike her own. Being cruel was not in his nature, unlike her cousin.

"Jeb, I thank you for anticipating my needs, but I don't require Lightning this morning. I believe I'll join Miss Montgomery on a stroll through the gardens."

Startled, Winnie protested, "I should not wish to delay your enjoyments, Mr. Dryden. I'm sure you would prefer a ride."

115

"A walk can be just as satisfying."

Jeb, Flynn, and Rupert's heads swung between her employer and her.

"But my walking pace is rapid—not at all what you are used to."

His brows lifted, but he replied smoothly, "I'll try not to slow your progress."

"It isn't necessary, sir."

Jeb, a lanky fellow, lifted his hat and wiped his brow. He gave a low whistle then made a cheeky grin.

She ignored it, disliking being the center of attention. Winnie couldn't imagine why Mr. Dryden was making such a pest of himself.

Her employer placed her hand atop his arm, practically purring, "I insist."

Sharply, she spoke and withdrew her hand. "I decline."

Rupert, the freckled lad, protested. "Miss Monty, I really think you ought to take your morning stroll with the captain."

Again, Mr. Dryden put her hand upon his forearm, murmured his thanks to Rupert, and hissed in her ear, "Must you be so stubborn?"

"I didn't ask for an escort, thank you very much!"

"You may walk with me as your escort or another groom, but you shall take a solitary walk this morning. Is that clear, Miss Montgomery?"

Flynn snorted, "I've no likin' to be a-walking maids in the daylight. Beg your pardon, ma'am."

Charles arrowed a silencing glare at the Scot.

"Come." Mr. Dryden said, resuming his grip on her elbow. "Please. I'll explain when we're alone. Everything all right, Flynn?"

"Yes, sir. But I'm warning ye now, we're bound for rain, ter be sure. Me knee aches. You'll be wanting to step lively."

Winnie gazed at the cloudless sky. "I doubt your forecast, Flynn. Looks to be a lovely day."

"It's a-comin', miss. Mind ye that. Be 'ere long 'fore luncheon." Flynn rubbed his knee as he made his prediction.

"Yes, I fear something's in the air," Mr. Dryden murmured, knifing an intense gaze toward both stable hands. "It

116

would behoove you to take all the necessary precautions you can *muster*."

Again, Winnie sensed something off-kilter in the conversation, as though another, entirely different meaning, lurked beneath the words, which eluded her.

Nodding his understanding to Mr. Dryden's murky message, Jeb waved them off. "Enjoy your walk."

They walked cross the cobble stones, the sound of their footsteps the only sound in an awkward silence. As Winnie reflected over the morning's events, her brow pleated. She had no idea the source for the mysterious disquiet in the stable yard, but her companion had said he'd explain once they were alone. With a slight shock, Winnie realized she believed him. Could it be that she was beginning to trust this rascal?

Her escort startled her by spreading an arm wide and declaring, "Isn't it a glorious, sunshiny day, Miss Monty?"

Torn between irritation and amusement for his filching of Rupert's moniker, Winnie didn't know how to respond. With her lips twitching, she replied with asperity, "Oh, fine, you horrid, smug, infuriating man—it *is* a blissful day."

Mr. Dryden raised his fore finger as his eyes gleamed with humor. "You failed to mention military hero."

In her best dead-pan voice, she said, "How you walk through doorways with such a swollen head is beyond me."

He patted her arm and searched her face with touching concern. "What troubles your sleep, Winsome?"

She cast him a sideways glance, startled by the familiarity.

"Please, call me Chas. Or Charles."

"Thank you, no, sir. It's not appropriate." She fixed her eyes straight ahead, ignoring his handsome profile.

"Calling me by my given name is the least of your present worries. It's time to forego formality." When she didn't reply, he coaxed, "Let some light in. Live a little."

She scrutinized him, gauging his sincerity, to find to her astonishment that he met her gaze. Reading humor, compassion, and something else in his eyes, she turned the matter over in her head. Did Mr. Dryden worry for her sake? He'd asked at the fairies pond, then again last night what troubled her. He must wish to know the reason for her disquiet. Knowing somebody cared about her well-being jolted her.

She smiled at her employer, glad to have made a friend.

He returned her smile.

She conceded, wagging her finger. "Fine, but I'll call you Charles, if that's acceptable with you? You may call me Winnie."

"Thank you, but I think I prefer the more accurate moniker of Winsome."

Despite herself, she blushed, pleased with his preference. She liked his the sound of his rich voice saying her name. "It's embarrassing, naturally, but Mama had her reasons for naming me that. Sir Vernon never quite approved."

Her companion's expression assumed a polite, bland mask. Winnie looked down, afraid she'd revealed too much.

"Do you ride, Winnie? Jeb informed me you daily visit the horses, so you must feel comfortable in their company. It would be my pleasure to provide you with a mount—once your arm heals, of course."

She stopped, mid-stride as her eyes flew wide open. "Really?"

"Really, truly." Twinkle in his brown eyes belied his stern tone.

A cold voice called from behind the shepherd statue. "I beg your pardon."

She whirled toward the intruder. Upon hearing that familiar, contemptible voice, a cold finger trailed Winnie's spine, banishing warmth and replacing it with a killing frost.

Leaning against the statue's base, Sir David tapped the sole of his boot with his riding crop. He watched Winnie's reaction, presenting a cavalier image, at odds with the malicious gleam in his eyes. Behind him a bay pawed at the ground, cleaving the tender soil. The horse snorted, steam rising from its nostrils.

Two days before, they had seen a rider on a bay horse. She'd argued that her cousin could not possibly know her whereabouts, but she cursed herself for not paying attention to those gut feelings of disquiet. Who else but Sir David had ever evoked such a reaction from her?

A near-whimper left her.

Charles' head snapped toward her.

"You!" she croaked.

"How delightful to see you again, dear cousin. I've missed you so much."

His voice, soft as a snake's hiss, created gooseflesh on her arms.

He approached the pair, murder in his eyes.

Winnie stepped closer to Charles, who pulled her behind him, as she had done with Arianna. Winnie welcomed the haven his body provided. Her cousin terrified her. A phantom pain rumbled through her arm so that it throbbed and ached where it'd been broken.

Sir David laughed without mirth. Sneering at her huddled form, his lip curled. "Shall I congratulate you on your recent…marriage?"

His dark eyes darted between her and Charles. "No? Engagement perhaps?"

"Miss Montgomery is my daughter's governess and under my protection," Charles warned.

Sir David clucked his tongue in that mocking way she so detested. "My, my, dear cousin. Cavorting with your employer? You'd do better to return to Stanhope and accept the arrangements I made for you."

"Never!"

Dark, pitiless eyes roved over her face and form, and Winnie hid behind her employer, disliking that feral gleam.

Beneath her fingers, she felt tension ripple through Charles. The muscles in those broad shoulders bunched as his hands made fists, but his anger somehow reassured her.

"Sir David Broomstead, at your service. Your…um, companion, seems reluctant to introduce us."

Certain the slight pause in addressing her as a companion had been intended as a slur, Winnie's cheeks burned. She buried her forehead between Charles' shoulder blades, gripping the sides of his wool jacket until her fingers cramped.

Remaining rooted to the spot, Charles gave a terse nod. "Charles Dryden. Perhaps you will explain why you're trespassing on my family's land?"

"Am I? I do beg your pardon. My wife and I are house guests of Mr. Peters of Landry House."

His words dropped like stones in the pit of her stomach. Winnie peered around Charles, staring at her cousin's charming façade. It wouldn't endure, she knew. Sooner or later, he'd reveal his vicious nature. She stepped closer to Charles, wishing she could melt into the weave of the fabric of his clothes.

"Is that right?"

Sir David spoke in honeyed tones, "Come, cousin. After all we've been through together, let's have a kiss, eh?"

"Don't touch me! And don't speak to me, either, you cur!"

His lips stretched into an upward curl. "You'll be sorry you said that, Winnie. Did you enjoy my gift, sweetings? I left it on the mounting blo—"

Charles moved so rapidly Winnie's brain couldn't comprehend what happened next. Cool air rushed in, followed by a crunching sound, a grunt, and then Sir David ended up sprawled on the ground.

"You damned coward! Get up!" Charles' reddened fist circled the air while he paced over her cousin's prostrate form. "Get up!"

Rubbing his jaw, Sir David languished instead on the ground then chuckled. "I think not. Your punch has a hearty helping of science behind it."

"Don't come onto this property again," Charles said through clenched teeth.

"I go where I please, Dryden. Nothing short of killing me will prevent that." Sir David spoke without emotion, but his words chilled her.

As though he wasn't surprised by that, Charles nod and returned in like manner, "Then it will be my privilege to oblige you. I repeat, don't come here again."

"Please," Winnie whispered, sickened by this talk of killing. "Please just go."

Testing his jaw, the baronet took his time before returning to his feet. He snatched his riding crop from the grass then saluted Winnie, murmuring, "Cousin."

She cast him a look of loathing.

He spun, re-mounted the bay then cantered off.

With her heart in her throat, she covered her mouth with a shaky hand. Her broken arm throbbed in its sling as she watched his departure.

Charles remained motionless until Sir David became a speck on the horizon. Finally he turned to her and asked, "Is he the reason for your nightmares?"

Bleakly, she nodded, unable to speak past the lump.

"He's your father's heir?"

Again she nodded.

"And he means you harm."

He didn't ask that last statement, merely summarized his conclusion. Winnie didn't nod or speak—the tightening of her throat made such impossible. She dashed moisture from her eyes and gulped in a lungful of air, trying to compose herself.

"Is he responsible for breaking your arm?"

Her head jerked. A wave of shame flooded her and she couldn't bear to let this man know how dishonorable her family was, so she stared at the ground instead.

"Winsome?"

The grass blurred. A strained voice she didn't recognize as her own answered, "Yes."

"Please tell me what happened."

Perhaps it was because he said 'please,' or perhaps it was the gentleness in his voice, but it proved her undoing. Her paltry attempts to maintain her composure were wasted. Like a dam bursting, she cried then found her head cradled against Charles. His arms went around her, pulling her closer into his embrace.

His warm body soothed her, he whispered words and sounds into her ear. They remained like that for the longest time, a tempting glimpse of eternity. Eventually her sobs subsided to an occasional hiccup. She dashed the tears from the corner of her eyes, dabbed her nose with the corner of her sling. He chuckled, reminding her of the impropriety of snuggling her employer. She stepped back, muttering something incomprehensible. With an inward grimace, she realized her embarrassment simply underscored her gaucheness.

Charles said nothing, allowing her out of his arms. He extracted his handkerchief, as he'd done before, and offered it in compassionate silence.

She smiled. She dabbed her eyes, wiped her nose, straightened her hair—all necessary, but also done to stall for more time. When she was sure she could speak without her voice cracking, she asked, "What did he mean by 'his gift'? Why did that make you hit him?"

"Oh, hell."

"Something about 'his gift' upset Rupert and the others, didn't it?"

Puffing out his cheeks, he then swore again. "Yes, you wretch, but I'm not yet ready to offer you that explanation, so you first, Winsome."

Staring into his eyes, she became aware that he would not be moved. "You are so stubborn!"

By a mere lift of a single eyebrow, Charles awaited her answer.

"He...he pulled me down the stairs at Stanhope."

"What?" The word left his mouth at gunshot speed.

"I tried to run away, but couldn't. He snagged my sash then jerked until I lost balance. I broke my arm when I tumbled down the stairs."

Charles' swift intake of breath unnerved her, but she continued in a rush. "I ran because he threatened to make me his mistress."

"*What?*" Without waiting for a reply, Charles let loose a hot string of expletives that could have melted the bronze statute under which they stood.

Winnie flinched, startled by his vehemence and vocabulary. "I should've killed him."

"Oh, no."

Standing with his hands on his hips, Charles bit out, "Oh, yes."

"You're the most impulsive—"

He smiled at her. A broad smile made of equal parts delight and affection. Affection? Confused, she shook her head then turned away. "I must leave, find another position."

122

She watched the smile transform into a scowl.

"Why on earth would you do that?"

"Because I'm not safe here. Sir David is evil, cruel. How he discovered my whereabouts, I may never know, but I must leave."

"A baronet's daughter does not run away," he chided.

"This one does."

"Running away would only make you vulnerable, more exposed," he argued.

She ignored him, ticking off her list of things to do on her fingers. "I must write to the employment agency, pack my bags. I'll need a reference."

"Winsome. Look at me." He caught her hand and lifted her chin.

Seeing the tender look in his eyes, Winnie caught her breath. Tingles spread from her hand and traveled up her arms. It had been so pleasant to be in his arms, but holding hands was lovely, too.

He took a deep breath then said in a rush, "I need a wife to sire an heir for the earldom. You need the protection of a husband. Why not marry?"

What did he say? She shook her head, imagining she'd misheard him. Her voice squeaked. "Each other?"

One corner of his mouth moved upward and his shoulders lost some of the tension he carried since leveling Sir David.

"Why, that's…that's…" She was at a loss for words. Meeting his gaze, she wondered why he would have made such an impulsive offer then the reason struck her. "You're just being kind, and I thank you for defending me, but we can't possibly marry."

"Why not?"

She frowned, hearing a peculiar tone in his question she couldn't name. "You don't wish to marry me. Not really."

"I do," he insisted, tightening his grip. "Think how practical it would be! You'd get to be a mother to Arianna and any other children we might have. I would provide for you so that you'd never have to be in service—" His words rushed out, each one stabbing her until she thought she'd become a sieve.

"Stop." Snatching her hand away, she spoke over the heavy lump re-lodged in her throat. "Our stations are totally unequal. It would be a misalliance from the very start."

"I don't care for that."

"Well, you should. I have no dowry, Mr. Dryden."

"I don't need your dowry."

That stumped her.

"I've been in service." She glanced at him, exasperation marking her tone.

"Why should that matter?"

"Because it *does*."

"Not to me it doesn't, and since you and I are the only ones who would be affected, why let that stop you from accepting my offer?"

She slammed her fist on her hip. "Why are you doing this?"

"I've already explained, but in case you weren't listening, allow me to—"

"No!"

"No?"

"No." Her hand shook as she tucked a loose strand behind her ear.

Charles' lips pressed together. After giving her a long, hard look, he tersely said, "Release me from my second condition."

"What?"

"The second condition, Winsome." Something wicked lurked in his voice, as he reached for her shoulders.

His knuckles were reddened from leveling her cousin. Her anger left in an instant. She examined his hand, saluting the gallant fist with a quick 'thank you' kiss.

He grew still.

"The hair cut? Don't be silly. I already rescinded it."

"Not that one. This one." The hoarseness in his voice caused her to raise startled eyes to his gaze.

In the next instant, his mouth covered hers. This was no sweet, light meeting of the lips. When she gasped in surprise, his tongue invaded her mouth, deepening the kiss. The suddenness of it surprised her. Winnie had never been kissed like this before.

Tingles and sparks spread throughout her. She reveled in the new experience. She kissed him back, matching his desire. Her response fed his then doubled back to her. Charles kissed her as if he'd been dying to do so for centuries. He moaned, kissing her eyelids, cheek, and throat as her fingers trailed through his silky, dark hair then massaged his nape.

She closed her eyes, giving into the pleasure his roving hands stirred sensation within her. She marveled how well they fit together. He cupped her bottom and pressed his hard body against her lower belly. Belatedly, she realized the significance of his hardness. Rather than being shocked, though, she was thrilled to discover the effect she had on him.

She wondered if they'd soon burst into flames. She wanted more of him, to feel his skin. Their garments had become too hot and cumbersome, all of a sudden.

Charles broke off the kiss, his chest heaving and his shirt tail untucked.

Good Lord! Did I do that?

He stepped back, allowing a whoosh of cool air between them. The man looked utterly shaken. It took a good long while for his breathing to return to regularity, much longer still for the stunned expression to leave his face.

Winnie watched, appalled and dismayed by her response. She had no idea she could behave in such a wanton fashion.

"Are you well? Did I hurt your arm?"

Dazed, she touched her broken arm, running her fingers along the sling. "I'm fine."

A lazy note of amusement entered his warm, rich voice, as he asked, "Which do you prefer? Having the banns read or marrying by special license? I'd have to travel to London, but otherwise it would take three weeks—"

Lowering her hand to her side, it balled into a fist as she declared, "We are not marrying!"

He stared at her. "Of course we are!"

"No. No amount of kissing changes the fact that it would be…unequal." Another reason for the inequality occurred to her. She gasped at that epiphany.

"Who cares about that? Not I! Can't you see that marrying me would be ideal? For both of us? I'd protect you and as sister-in-law to the Earl of Northampton, your cousin would not dare harm you again. You can't deny there's a very strong attraction between us."

"No. No, it won't do. I must leave." She whirled around, needing to place some distance between them. Her heart hammered in double time.

He was right on her heels.

She could practically feel his scowl burning into her back. "You're not leaving. We will marry."

Winnie hastened her pace and glanced over her shoulder.

Charles wore a grim expression, storm clouds in his gaze.

She ducked her head, fervently hoping he hadn't guessed her secret—the one which had just been revealed to her.

Chapter 12

It took Charles a while to label the emotions roiling through him. He first recognized elation, so started analyzing that. Gratified and astonished, he'd discovered the prim, feisty governess kissed like a dream. Her initial hesitation assured him of her innocence, but as soon as her tongue tangled with his, he knew she'd keep up with him every step of the way. He hadn't been prepared for the volcanic eruption of lust. It nearly overwhelmed him. Even he had under-estimated his attraction to Winsome. He wanted to throw his head back and whoop with joy.

The baronet's presence heralded the second emotional revelation: terror. Charles wasn't afraid of Sir David—the idea was ludicrous, but the baronet terrified Winsome and that wouldn't do. Why, she'd hidden behind him like a frightened rabbit. What she suffered at Sir David's hands! He understood better why she'd insisted on her bothersome 'conditions' of employment and confirmed his suspicions regarding her cool demeanor. She donned it as a mantle, like a Crusader wore his chain mail. Winsome protected herself with the only weapons she had available, and she'd been forced to do so because the ones who should have protected her failed her.

Sir David's lustful gaze frequently rested upon Winsome, much to Charles' chagrin. The dolt didn't bother hiding his prurient thoughts. A man totally without honor, to be threatening his dependent in such a manner. Then to intentionally strike at Winsome when she'd refused him? He wasn't sure his expansive vocabulary could adequately describe his view of Sir David.

He stared at the female striding ahead at a brisk pace. How her strength, courage, and determination got bundled into such an appealing package, Charles didn't know, but a grin inched across his face.

He, too, began making lists. His was a shopping list, which differed from Winsome's plans for a leave-taking. Purchase an engagement ring, commission negligees—the see-through kind, buy a few bottles of champagne.

At the base of the sweeping staircase, she paused. "I regret to leave you so soon, but I'll request a letter of character, sir, and my wages."

"No." Once more he guided her by the healthy elbow, relieved she offered no resistance. Rather than re-entering the house, he returned with her to the stables. He cast her a sideways glance and tossed her own words back at her. "I won't do it."

She blinked, unwittingly echoing his response. "What do you mean you won't do it?"

He smiled. She made his heart sing without even trying. "You're not leaving my employ."

His bald statement was not met with a rush of gratitude, proving him to be a foolish optimist. In fact, Winsome's face turned stony.

"I can't afford to let you go. Rather than running away, I suggest you watch and learn, Miss Montgomery." He signaled the groomsmen to gather together.

Tapping her toe against the cobblestones, Winsome's hand went to her hip and her slender eyebrows arched. Charles was growing to hate that look of hers. It spelled intransigence on her part and he didn't hold much confidence in his abilities to turn it aside.

"Flynn! Jeb! Ah, there you are, Rupert," Charles greeted the stable hands.

"Did you enjoy your walk, Miss Monty?" The stable lad asked, toeing the dirt.

Flustered by the simple question, Winsome stammered something before Charles cut her off. "No, Rupert, she did not. It appears we have an unwelcome stranger in our midst, gentlemen. Mr. Peters of Landry House is hosting a house party and one of his guests—disagreeable fellow named Sir David, Baronet of Stanhope, wandered onto our land. We met him at the shepherd statue. Be on the look-out for his horse, a bay with white stockings on its front legs. Sir David has black hair, dark eyes, and stands not quite six feet tall. Did I miss anything, Miss Montgomery?"

"N-no."

"Good." Charles nodded then re-addressed the stable hands. "The man is dangerous. One of you must accompany Miss Montgomery on her morning walks if I'm not available."

"Yes, sir," Jeb said, tugging his hat's brim, but without his usual smile in place.

Giving the governess a reassuring nod, Flynn said, "Me pleasure, lass."

Charles stared at her until she squirmed. "You are not to walk without an escort. Is that clear, Miss Montgomery?"

"What are you doing, Mr. Dryden?"

"It's called mounting a defense, rather than beating a retreat. Now observe military strategy at work." He faced the three males. "Flynn? Jeb? Take a pistol—"

"A pistol?"

He put his finger in his ear and wiggled it, trying to ease the discomfort her shrillness created.

"That's not necess—"

"It is," he said, squashing her objection. "Carry a pistol along with you and keep a loaded blunderbuss in the stables until further notice. I'll inform the footmen within to help you in patrolling the grounds in four-hour shifts. Flynn, arrange a schedule for every available man to serve guard duty, including myself. Be on the look-out for the man. Shoot if you have to."

"What?"

Charles asked the stable lad, "Rupert, do you know how to shoot?"

"Yes, sir!"

Flynn's beefy hand clapped onto Rupert's shoulder. "You think Cook's fowls drop from the sky? That'd be Rupert's bird ye be dining on, nine times of ten."

"Really?" Charles smiled at the blushing lad. "I'm impressed, Rupert."

The lad owned that he liked hunting. "Jeb taught me. He's a crack shot."

"He taught me, too," Charles agreed, glancing at his old mentor.

"I ain't so old that I don't remember those lessons, sir," Jeb said, his usual grin back in place.

"Flynn, see to it that Rupert's assigned the first watch."

Having heard enough, a much paler Winsome stepped forward and slashed her hand through the air. "No. I absolutely forbid it! I don't want anyone getting shot."

"You voice those objections quite strenuously."

"Yes."

"Do you believe that Sir David will return? That he poses a risk to yourself and others at Canon Ashby?"

"Well...er...that is to say..." She heaved a sigh. "Yes, yes. He's a horrid person, who enjoys being cruel."

"Well, since I already divined that, we will do better to prepare for the worst Sir David offers. Come now, let us return to the house." So saying, he reclaimed her elbow and escorted her from the cobblestone yard.

The Scotsman winked at Charles. When Rupert turned away, Charles mouthed something to Flynn and the groom nodded his agreement.

"You told him not to let Rupert shoot him, didn't you?"

"But of course."

Escorting the tight-lipped woman into the manor house, Charles was delighted by her show of spunk. That fiery temper made him want to kiss her again, see if he could soften that primed mouth and hear again those delightful moans she made in the back of her throat.

Fearing to sound eager, he asked in the most off-handed fashion he could, "Have you decided yet to be my wife?"

He could have grown two extra heads by the way Winnie boggled at him.

"Are you mad?"

Inspecting his fingernails, he drawled, "Well then, how long will you need before you decide to marry me?"

She stared at him, her mouth forming an opening wide enough to house a family of sparrows. "You must be mad."

"Darling," he prompted, thanking the devilish imp which had taken residence on his shoulder for this latest suggestion. "As your betrothed, I insist we finish our sentences with endearments. Given that your greatest wish will be to please me, you should say, 'Are you mad, *darling*?' or 'You must be mad, *darling*.'"

As she shook her head in stunned amazement, Charles' mouth burst into an undisciplined smile again. She made him laugh—he couldn't help himself.

"Good Lord, you are a regular candidate for Bedlam. That is, you're a candidate for Bedlam, *darling*." She batted her lashes at the end of this declaration and feigned a look of adoration.

Basking in the glow this look engendered, he crossed his arms and allowed his gaze to roam over the curves of her face and figure. Now that he'd held her in his arms, he wanted to do it again.

"What on earth would people say? Why would the Honorable Charles Dryden—formerly a captain in the army—marry his employee, a poor baronet's daughter, forced into service?"

Before he could answer these considerations were too stupid to matter, she pressed her hand to her cheek. "Why, they'd assumed I snared you in some devious, underhanded scheme!"

"'The lady doth protest too much, methinks,'" he murmured.

"Surely you must see this misalliance—have you no notion of the disparity between our stations?"

Raising his voice so he might drown out her opposition, he declared, "I don't give a damn for such things. My first marriage was based upon such stupid considerations and Vivian and I were miserable from start to finish."

"There's no guarantee our marriage would be better," she argued with her sassy, delectable mouth.

"Of course it would."

Resisting the urge to kiss her again to prove his point, he ticked off the points on his hand. "One, I need to marry and produce an heir. Two, you need a protector. Three, you'd make the perfect mama for Arianna. Four, Sir David has probably announced to half the county we're having an affair."

131

The whites of Winnie's eyes showed as she choked, "What?"

A grim line formed his lips and he urged her to think about it. "He lost the skirmish today—I probably shouldn't have flattened him like that, but there it is. He'll now try to embarrass us. What better way than to start the rumor we're having an affair in my ancestral home? You wouldn't stand a chance to get another post in Northamptonshire."

"That's despicable!"

"It's called 'harassing the rear flank.' Would you expect anything less from the cretin?"

She slumped against a wall, all the fight draining from her. "Was there a fifth reason? If so, please tell."

He looked at his fully-splayed hand. "Fifth? Darling, reason one had two parts, so..."

"The marriage *and* the heir." She raised her gaze toward heaven, as if seeking patience from On High.

His lips twitched. In a flash of insight, Charles suspected in the next moment Winsome could either weep or laugh hysterically, depending on the direction the wind blew. Nothing in his twenty-nine years prepared him for handling a woman in such a mood—certainly, his time in the Army gave him no inkling. So, when he heard Will's approaching footsteps, he greeted his brother with relief.

"Good morning, Miss Montgomery," Lord Northampton sketched her a salute.

She choked out, "Is it? Is it *really*, I wonder?" Then Winsome Montgomery gathered her voluminous skirts and left them on the stairwell.

Shocked at her cryptic reply, Will gave him a sidelong glance. Charles shrugged, as though he, too, had been mystified and hid his smile. What was there about the woman that made him so *damned* happy?

They entered the breakfast room and Bertram poured his lordship his daily cup of coffee while another footman selected items from the side table for their meals. The brothers sat in silence as they were waited upon, but when the last servant left the room, Will asked off-handedly, "What's upset the Icicle?"

Charles dabbed the corner of his mouth with the napkin, refolded it then said, "You must congratulate me. The Icicle and I are to wed." He picked up his napkin to blot the tablecloth, now speckled in coffee spots, sprayed from Lord Northampton's mouth.

Northampton swatted his brother's hand, snatched the napkin from Charles and finished the chore. He gave a nervous laugh then confessed, "For a moment there, I thought you said you were to wed…"

His smile unrepentant, Charles assured Will, "That's what I said."

With great consternation, the Earl blinked. Then he picked up his fork and resumed eating. Chewing his eggs as he considered his next words, Will ended the silence by testing the waters. "I apologize if I pressured you to re-marry, Chas. There's no need to buckle yourself to the first decent woman who crosses your path."

"Oh, for pity's sake!" Charles scoffed. "When have I ever acted the martyr?"

Will nodded, agreeing with that. "Then you *wish* to marry the Ici…ehem. Beg pardon. I mean, Miss Montgomery?

Charles leveled a warning glare at Will's slip of the tongue.

"I do." He chuckled. "See how naturally the vow springs from me?"

They finished the meal before Charles recalled the matter of Sir David. "Winnie's cousins, the Baronet and Lady of Stanhope, are staying at Landry House with Peters. I met Sir David in the south gardens. The man's a blighter of the first order. I've ordered our men to carry weapons in case he should be sighted on our land again."

Will's fork halted in mid-air, hovering above the plate of kippers. "Oh?"

"Yes. He demanded Winsome become his mistress. When she refused, he caused her to fall down the stairs. That's how she broke her arm."

"My God!" The Earl's fork clattered to the tabletop.

"Yes, mine, too." Charles continued, "The man's unstable. This morning, Rupert found a mutilated barn cat pinned to the mounting block where Winnie would have seen it. Fortunately, we hid it in the nick of time, but when the dastard admitted he'd done it, I knocked him down."

"He admitted it?"

"Taunted, more like."

Lord Northampton gave a low whistle, agreeing, "The man must be unhinged."

"Yes. Had I known beforehand the insult he'd given her, I'd have done more than knock him down."

"I believe you." Will raised his coffee cup in a silent toast.

"Her father was a ne'er-do-well, too. Cheated her out of her dowry."

"What's this?"

"Sir Vernon gambled it away, I gather."

"Now you propose to be the errant knight and rescue the damsel in distress, eh? I can see how her broken arm adds to that appealing, pathetic picture."

"Hah! Fat lot you know! The broken arm is a damned nuisance."

"So you're not on a crusade then?"

"What the devil, Will? Do you actually imagine the war changed me so much?"

His brother said nothing then slowly, as if the words were pulled from him, "It has changed you, though. You would agree to that, wouldn't you?"

Charles nodded. "The attack at Busaco shook me. I will bear the scars from that bloody day the rest of my life, but I wasn't eager to sell my commission and become a gentleman farmer and father, either. You see, I had no experience in those roles."

"You'll do fine, Chas."

"I hope so." He flashed Will a smile, grateful for the vote of confidence. He dispatched the remainder of his meal before saying, "Miss Montgomery requires a husband's protection, and I want to protect her. Can you understand that?"

"I do."

"Careful who you say that phrase to," Charles ribbed his older brother. "I'd already decided to marry her before this morning's walk, but this latest development will force me to rush my timetable for wooing."

"You? You were going to woo Miss Montgomery?"

"Certainly."

Ruminating on this latest revelation, Will asked, "Tell me, Chas, *when* did you decide to marry Miss Montgomery?"

"It's been coming on for a while now."

"I see." The lord cleared his throat and flushed. "Beg pardon, but *why* have you decided to marry her?"

Buttering the last piece of toast, Charles ignored his brother's baffled tone. "She's kind, tactful, and intelligent. I like her sense of humor. She loves Arianna, which must always be a point in a step-mother's favor, I should think," he said before polishing off his toast. Speaking with his mouth full and his eyes twinkling with devilry, he said, "And she kisses like a dream."

Pointing his fork at his brother, Will stated, rather than asked, "You esteem her." Pleased to have solved that mystery, the Earl moved his empty plate aside and patted his belly.

Charles halted his chewing as he considered the matter. Finally, he swallowed the toast then nodded, agreeing with Will's conclusion. "Yes, I esteem and respect her."

"How fortunate," Lord Northampton murmured, a gleam in his eyes as he picked up his cup.

"Oh, I almost forgot, Will. She doesn't wish to marry me."

Will choked on his coffee then wiped the dribble from his chin, grumbling, "Don't know why I bother drinking anything whilst conversing with you."

"No." Charles scowled at his empty plate. "She'd do much better as my wife than as a mere governess. Can't understand her resistance."

"Well, you did say she was intelligent…"

Charles' head snapped round upon hearing his brother's facetious comment. In his most determined voice, he declared, "I mean to marry her; it will not be a misalliance."

"It's irregular, but not unheard of, marrying a governess. Her birth is suitable."

He threw his napkin down. "She keeps harping on the match being unequal. As if I needed her dowry."

"True. I say, Chas, where are you going?" His head swung around to view Charles leaving the breakfast room.

135

"I have to purchase a ring, don't I?" He stood, scratching the back of his head. "Should probably arrange some nicer dresses to be made up—what colors do you suggest for Winsome? Red? Rose?"

"Anything save brown, darling brother," Will drawled then added, "Must've been some kiss."

Charles grinned as he left the breakfast room, and he wore that grin for the rest of the day.

Chapter 13

"Miss Montgomery? May I interrupt Arianna's lessons?"

Winnie couldn't have been more surprised to see Lord Northampton at the door. Recovering from the shock, she bowed. "Certainly, my lord."

The Earl entered, approached Arianna's desk, and examined his niece's slate. "Ah, I see you're practicing your letters. Very good, Arianna. Very good."

The girl giggled. "How are you, Uncle Will?"

He cupped the back of her head and smiled at her. "I am well. Do you like rainy days?"

"No, not really."

"Me, neither."

They stared at the window, watching the downpour then sighed in unison. Flynn's weather prediction had proven true.

The four-year old's eyes sparkled with delight. "Have you come to play with me, uncle?"

"No, Arianna. In fact, I wish to speak with Miss Montgomery about your progress. Would you please take Juju to the kitchens? Cook has biscuits for you both."

The pronouncement filled Winnie with dread, fearing she was to be chastised, possibly dismissed. She nibbled her bottom lip. His lordship must have learned she kissed his brother. Perhaps he discovered the baronet tracked her to Canon Ashby? Either way, Winnie was sure his presence did not bode well for her.

A cold realization struck Winnie's midi-section. She didn't wish to leave the Drydens. Until this moment, she'd been so preoccupied with making plans for departure and relocation, that it hadn't struck her how much she loved being part of this family.

The earl was kind, the countess amusing, Juju welcomed her and Winnie loved Arianna as if she were her own daughter. Of Charles, she was becoming much too fond, her frequent mental meanderings often touched on his generosity, humor or handsomeness. Or his fine shoulders.

She gave herself a mental shake. It was stupid and pointless to dream of her employer. He'd offered to marry her in an impulsive, gallant decision, but he never once spoke of finer emotions. It wouldn't have mattered if he did. Granted, he'd not been drunk since the night of that debacle of a dinner, so she could acquit him on that charge, but she mustn't develop a *tendre* for Charles. He was still a womanizer and gambler, or at least, she believed him to be.

She sniffed, hoping it would escape the Earl's notice. She turned her mind to practical details, lest she become a watering pot. Would she receive any wages? She would need some funds to tide her over until she found new employment. Would Lady Northampton provide a recommendation or dismiss her without a character for having kissed her son in the south garden? Would she think Winnie a trollop, who set her cap at Charles? Perhaps she was a trollop—kissing Charles had been the highlight of her life thus far.

Winnie nodded to Arianna and went to the adjoining door to call the nurse. "Juju? Will you come here, please? Lord Northampton desires you to escort Arianna to the kitchens."

The African woman finished straightening the nursery and came into the school room, wearing a broad smile, which revealed a strong, healthy set of startling-white teeth.

"G'afternoon, Master Will," she said with a shallow curtsey, her arthritic knees preventing anything deeper.

Winnie smiled at the earl being called 'Master Will,' as though he were still a lad in short pants, but she supposed having been nursemaid to him, Juju was beyond the formalities which applied to the other servants. The earl certainly didn't seem to mind; in fact, both brothers held their nanny in high esteem.

Winnie sat on the window seat, plumping a decorative, embroidered pillow, and cracked the window to allow for cooling air. She inhaled, letting the sweet smell of rain calm her.

138

The girl collected her dolly, tucking Miss Lucille into the crook of her arm. "Uncle Will, when my lessons are finished, will you play spillikins with me?"

"Yes, poppet, but I warn you, I feel mighty lucky today."

Arianna swayed, setting her skirts awhirl so that its fabric rustled. "Maybe I will win."

He drawled, "Dubious, dear niece."

She answered in giggles and grins. Taking the nursemaid's hand, Arianna informed her, "We're going to eat biscuits now, Juju. Did you know that?"

After they'd left the school room, Lord Northampton turned to her. Winnie motioned him to take a seat in her customary chair. He sat and dropped his bony elbows to his knobby knees. From the benevolence in his gaze, he seemed genuinely concerned for her welfare. That demeanor confirmed Winnie would soon be evicted from Canon Ashby. Why else would Lord Northampton look so kindly upon her? She drew a breath to steady her nerves.

Running away had been her first impulse when she saw Sir David. The idea of leaving wrenched her, but it would be unbearable if she were asked to leave. The inside of her nose began to sting. Winnie willed herself not to cry. It was so unlike her.

"I understand Baronet Stanhope poses a threat to you, Miss Montgomery."

Startled at his unexpected observation, Winnie stammered, "Y—yes, my lord."

"You do realize, don't you, that I am the local magistrate?"

"Yes?" The window seat upon which she rested seemed to tilt. She clutched the small pillow, using it as an anchor.

"That I sit in the House of Lords?"

She nodded.

"Should you feel discomforted by Sir David's presence, you must tell me. I will issue an arrest warrant for him."

Shocked at such a generous offer, she hardly knew what to say. "Thank you, my lord. You are very good."

"I am glad you think so, but I ask you to withhold your fine sentiments until I am at the end, for I doubt if my next words will please you half so much."

Deflated, Winnie's shoulders shrank and she mumbled, "No, but I shan't make a fuss. I do ask, however, that I receive some share of wages. If you please, I'd also very much like a recommendation letter for my next post."

"What?" Lord Northampton shook his head. Then his mouth twitched in a way that reminded Winnie of his younger brother. "No, Miss Montgomery. I fear you mistake me."

She pushed the pillow from her lap.

He shifted in the chair, one hand resting on his knee with the elbow bent. "My brother informs me he has proposed—"

"Oh, no, my lord. That's a hum! He hasn't *really* proposed."

"Has he not?"

"Well, he has," Winnie reassured the lord before adding, "but he didn't mean it. He thought to help me out of a pinch, you see. Nothing more."

His chin rested near his chest before he chided, "I fear, Miss Montgomery, gentlemen don't propose for those reasons. Didn't Charles provide you with…um…sufficient impetus to consider his suit?"

"Oh." Winnie's forefinger pressed against her bottom lip. "Why, he did mention his reasons for marrying, but I don't…"

"You believe him to be insincere?"

Winnie frowned. Plenty of labels flitted through her mind regarding Charles Dryden, but insincerity wasn't one of them.

Lord Northampton, seeing her hesitation, prodded, "Perhaps you should consider his offer? I don't believe he's a repulsive candidate for marriage."

Jerking to a standing position, she snatched up the small pillow from the window seat, twirling it between her hands. Her face softened as she recalled his haunting confessions at the fairies pond, sipping warmed milk in the kitchen at midnight, the splendor of his left hook. "No, my lord, not that. Granted, Charles is brave. And kind." She frowned, owing it to her conscience to be thorough in her assessment. "He's rather endearing—"

Lord Northampton's eyebrows spiked, but he leaned forward, listening.

Her cheeks heated as she recalled an earth-shattering kiss.

The Earl's brows disappeared into his hairline.

She scrutinized the pillow before tossing it aside. "Mr. Dryden never meant to propose to me, my lord. He was being gallant. Furthermore, I won't be drawn into a loveless marriage."

The gentleman stood and straightened his waistcoat. "My brother holds you in high regard, Miss Montgomery. I have it from his own lips he esteems and respects you."

"He…he does?"

He strolled to the window and rested his palm against the frame, looking upon the rain-splattered pane. "At any rate, I think it best were you to act as my brother's betrothed at least until this Sir David fellow is no longer a threat—for your own safety, naturally. Consider it a charade with you posing as a fiancée, assuming a disguise for your own protection. Sir David may be vicious, but he's probably not foolish. An aggressive hunter will target a straggler because it's easy prey. If you're deemed to be a member of the Dryden family—or near enough as to make no difference, you're part of our herd, as it were."

"A pretend fiancée?"

"Yes. A secret, pretend fiancée."

Winnie tapped her mouth. "That would allow me to release him from the engagement once Mr. Peters' house party has concluded. Then Sir David and Lady Broomstead will return to Stanhope."

"Yes, quite."

"You must know I am well aware that an actual marriage between Charles and me would be preposterous."

"And why is that, Miss Montgomery?"

"The difference in our stations, my lord."

"Not an insurmountable obstacle. As the second son to an earldom, he has wider latitude to marry."

"Of course," she agreed without changing her opinion. "However, I cannot help but think such would be a misalliance."

"Again, I must beg for your reasoning."

Rather impatiently, for she wearied of the Earl's bovine expression, she bit out, "I'm his daughter's governess, your lordship."

"I am aware."

"Some may say I am well past my prime."

"Then they would be foolish beyond permission. Besides, you're years younger than my brother, so…" He lifted one shoulder.

"I have no dowry."

"Charles has no need of it. He inherited a tidy sum and a substantial estate from his maternal grandfather." He smiled as though he knew he'd demolished every one of her objections.

For the first time that day, Winnie faced the real reason for her reluctance. How could she even pretend to marry Charles when their feelings were so lopsided? That's what she'd meant by their unequal positions. Could she bare it if the rascal didn't reciprocate her affection? For the past five years, Sir Vernon had never allowed thoughts of his daughter's well-being to interfere with his pleasure. Taking a husband who'd treat her without consideration would be blindingly stupid.

"It's unthinkable."

"Consider this, Miss Montgomery." He took her hand, brought it to his lips, and kissed the air above the knuckles. "You wouldn't actually have to marry Chas. The betrothal need only be for show to convince your cousin that you are not without friends, that you are not unprotected and at his mercy."

Frowning, she massaged her broken arm as Lord Northampton urged, "Safety in numbers, Miss Montgomery."

His lordship made it sound so practical.

She was alone in the world, save for the Dobsons and the Drydens. Her former butler and housekeeper couldn't shelter or rescue her, but the earl's family could. The phrase, 'Needs must when the devil drives,' returned to mock her. Surely, for the sake of her own safety, she could quell these fanciful, romantic notions of her employer? She was a woman grown, not a ninny hammer schoolgirl.

Winnie took a deep breath as she made an earth-moving decision. "Put that way, my lord, it's difficult to refuse. I shall be your brother's temporary, secret, pretend fiancée. It is a good solution for me and Charles should not come to any harm because of it, true?"

"It's ideal." He reassured her before confessing, "I must warn you, however, that I don't wish to alarm Mama. She and Arianna should be protected from Sir David, so, upon reflection, your engagement should appear authentic, not as a smokescreen. If Mama suspected otherwise, it would take her but a step to wondering about the contrivance. A short step from that and her peace of mind would flee."

"Oh." Winnie's fingertips massaged her temple. "No, I wouldn't wish Lady Northampton to worry about Sir David and certainly Arianna shouldn't know of such sordidness."

He bowed. "I thank you, ma'am. I knew I could rely upon your valiant discretion."

"Still, to behave as Charles' real fiancé…don't you think that would anger the countess, as well?"

"Why would it?"

"It's rather presumptuous of me."

"My dear, Mama has wanted Charles to get leg-shackled this past age. She'll be delighted to see progress toward that goal."

"Fake progress," she corrected. "And won't she be cross once she learns it's been phony, start to finish?"

"Doubtful, but if I miscalculate, I'll smooth over troubled waters, telling Mama this was her sons' ideas to keep you safe. She can't argue with that."

Satisfied with that answer, Winnie nodded. "I wouldn't want her to think I've tricked her."

A brief image of Charles came to her. If she accepted his impulsive proposal, tempered now to a façade, could she bear to see his relief? For reasons she didn't care to examine, she knew his reaction would hurt.

"Lord Northampton, would you—if it's not too undignified, please inform Mr. Dryden that I shall accept his proposal in the provisional manner we've discussed? I believe he may welcome such news."

Tilting his head, Lord Northampton considered this request. A slow smile stretched across his thin face before he assured her, "You may rely upon *my* valiant discretion, Miss Montgomery."

Chapter 14

After writing a sharp note to their neighbor, Mr. Peters, to request that his guests not wander onto Dryden property, Charles rode to the town of Northampton. During the ride, he became drenched, having forgotten to wear an overcoat. He felt impatient to be gone and in a rush to return. In truth, he felt apprehensive leaving Winsome alone for any length of time.

He made livery arrangements for Lightning, leaving the stallion to enjoy a dry stall, feed, and water then he searched out the tavern, glad to drink its heady ale while he stood by the fire, drying his garments.

His first purchase was a ring—an oval-shaped topaz trimmed in diamonds. He cursed himself for not having presented Winsome with a ring when he proposed, but he hoped she'd overlook his mistake. He'd been married before—he knew how important such things were to women. Winsome would be married once, he vowed with surprising fierceness, and he wanted the experience to be perfect. He congratulated himself on finding a handsome stone which matched her eyes.

His time at the dressmaker's wasn't half as easy. Purchasing a trousseau for his betrothed was dicey. The announcement of their pending wedding might not be sufficient to disabuse society from deeming her a light skirt. Unless related, a single man could not buy garments for an unmarried woman and Charles wanted to uphold Winsome's reputation. She might have once believed he was a womanizer, but she'd soon discover he had a care for her. To that end, he invented a familial connection between them.

Any military commander worth his salt had a plan of attack, so Charles gave the situation some thinking as he left the jewelry store. When he entered the dressmaker's shop, he mounted a brash offense.

"Good day, sir." A friendly, chubby, clerk greeted him in the near-empty shop. Bolts of fabrics were displayed on tables, along with gloves, fans, and reticules. The woolen and silk stockings were discreetly display along the back wall, hidden from voyeurs.

From his superior height, he stared down the poor clerk until she paled. Her reaction made him feel miserable, but there was no help for it. If he was to acquire new clothing for Winsome, he had to be ruthless.

His plan succeeded. The clerk stammered and stumbled over her words, "Beg pardon. I'll just fetch Madame Starling." She scurried away in a quick exit, leaving him stranded in the middle of the boutique, which was what he'd wanted—or so he tried to convince himself as he avoided the curious gazes of the other shoppers.

Charles paced the small area, inspecting their wares and trying not to reveal his mortification. He wished he had a quizzing glass; in the regular course of events, he despised affectations, but such would have been a handy prop in this farce.

A stout, middle-aged woman emerged from the fitting area. Dressed in black, she presented a daunting picture. Injecting a smidgeon of interest into her cold expression, she curved his lips. How had he thought Winsome could be the Silver Icicle when Madame Glacier stood before him?

"How may I help you, sir?"

Charles sensed a backbone made of steel. Madame Starling would make a valued accomplice if she agreed to his charade. Pleased that nobody had seen him in these parts for the past five years, he thought to take extra care and provided a fake name.

Better to be hanged as a lion than a lamb, he used his supercilious voice. "Yes, I'm Lord Whittles. My second cousin once removed—" he made a regal wave to indicate the connection was unimportant. "Has unexpectedly come to visit and the poor child requires suitable clothing. She'll need a ball gown, several

145

walking dresses, a riding habit, and half a dozen day dresses." He rattled off terms he'd seen while reviewing Vivian's modiste bills. "Oh, and stays and petticoats, too, I imagine. She will require adequate nighttime attire," he added as an afterthought. If he never saw Winnie in that blasted flannel robe, it'd be too soon.

Madame Starling's wary demeanor did not ebb. Glancing behind Mr. Dryden, she asked, "And where is this cousin, might I inquire, sir?"

"As you can observe, my good woman, she is not present. She's convalescing and I have come to fetch a new wardrobe in hopes of enticing her from the sick bed."

The faint rumble of thunder was heard in the distance and he hoped Zeus wouldn't fuss over these last clankers he told. Lord knows, worse lies had been spoken for far less noble reasons.

Two shrewd, hazel eyes narrowed upon him as the dressmaker considered her next response. While she hesitated, Charles pulled the pouch of coins from his coat and placed a sovereign across her palm. "For your discretion and haste."

That guided the woman's decision.

"Yes, my lord. Come right this way." Madame Starling led "the lord" into a private receiving area and ordered the frightened clerk to bring swatches, pattern-books, and tea. Her innocent countenance threw him off-guard when she inquired, "Have you a list of her measurements, Lord—I beg your pardon, did you say Lord Witless?"

By some miracle, he maintained an impassive expression. "The accent's on the first syllable—Whittles."

Her nod, obsequious and insincere, commenced their partnership.

"I require her measurements."

"You'll have to approximate, ma'am, for my cousin can't attend a fitting."

"Could I send an assistant to her for measurements?"

"Uh. No. No, thank you."

Madame Starling gave him a narrow look before being distracted by the clerk who arrived with the tea tray.

"Thank you, Janice."

Another assistant, carrying swatches and pattern books followed the plump, shy clerk who poured the tea.

Charles stood, indicating "his cousin's" height by tapping his hand to his shoulder. "She's not short, but she's no long Meg, either."

"I see." Madame Starling measured the distance from the floor to his hand and jotted it in a notepad. She then returned to her chair and sipped, thinking of a solution. Whispering an aside, Madame Starling asked, "My lord, if you would be so kind as to—discreetly, mind you—inspect my clerk, Janice, and tell me whether any of her…um…dimensions match those of your cousin's."

If his mama spied him now, she'd box his ears, no matter that he was a grown man of nine-and-twenty. Flushing, Charles nodded.

"Janice, be a dear, won't you, and fetch me that bolt of fabric from the bottom shelf?"

He inspected the beleaguered clerk's bottom, displayed in the performance of that particular chore. Charles shuddered then shook his head.

Madame Starling arched a brow.

"Too wide," Charles muttered, imagining his Harrow head-master caning him for this morning's work after his mama boxed his ears. His collar tightening, threatening to strangle him. "Margaret!"

The dressmaker's assistant, the one who brought the swatches and pattern books, re-appeared. As tall and lean as the other clerk, Janice, was short and stocky, the comparison struck him as one of extremes. The tape measure dangled from Margaret's neck and a dozen pins were stuck through her cuffs. "Yes, ma'am?" She squinted in Charles' direction, fidgeting with her thick spectacles.

"Please draw those drapes for us, child."

Once Margaret's back was turned, a chord struck Charles' memory. "Now that you mention it, perhaps in the…ah…eh…"

"Derriere?" Madame Starling's mouth twitched as though she struggled to keep her smile breaking forth.

He flashed the woman an ornery grin and they fell into the game with enthusiasm. By means of shrewd observation or other

147

downright contrivance, the twosome discerned Winsome's bosom matched the plump Janice's, the clerk. Her waist the size as another customer's, who Madame Starling assured him, wore stays.

"She appears to be happily proportioned," Madame Starling noted. "Your cousin, that is."

Oh yes, his mama would box his ears, his schoolmaster would cane him, and Winsome—God forbid—would wring his neck if today's outing came to light.

Well aware the dressmaker didn't believe his cover story, Charles ignored her sauciness. So long as she turned out a new wardrobe for Winsome and was discreet about it, he rather thought this association could be beneficial for everyone involved.

Next came a rather heated discussion regarding the selection of fabrics. Charles preferred crimsons, scarlets, and cherry-reds whereas Madame Starling declared a wardrobe should vary in its palette. After revealing his cousin was a woman of two-and-twenty who possessed vivid blue eyes and pale blonde hair, the dressmaker steered him toward jewel tones, incorporating sapphire blue and emerald green.

They compromised and agreed to use red silk for a ball gown, which would have gold embroidery on the sleeves and hem. Charles left the embroidery design to Margaret's discretion, but insisted the gown's neckline be cut low, but not too low.

Madame Starling approved.

The day dresses, Madame Starling insisted, should be pale and made of muslin or lawn with empire waists. They squabbled whether a lavender pelisse coordinated with the periwinkle lawn she selected, but in the end, Charles capitulated. Madame Starling sent Janice to the milliner's to purchase on approval a straw chipped bonnet decorated with a lavender ribbon. Once Charles saw the crowning touch on the outfit, he became confident that Madame Starling would dress his Winnie in flattering style.

They both agreed to use navy velvet for the riding habit. A jabot blouse with lace cuffs completed that particular ensemble and again, Janice produced a navy hat with a white plume which would curve along the jawline. At the end of two hours, a great deal had been accomplished, but more odds and ends still required sorting.

Although he'd stood his ground in the face of cavalry marches, Charles did not have the fortitude to outlast this assault. Cross-eyed from viewing so many patterns, he abdicated to Madame Starling the selection of folderols. He would send his man to collect the items next week.

"I can't possibly have this order ready in a week! Two weeks, perhaps…" Madame Starling scowled.

"When's the next assembly?" he asked, referring to the local dances held in Northampton.

"Full moon's April 8th," she told him.

"Fine. Have the ball gown ready for the assembly then send word as the rest is finished. We can have it delivered in stages, in trunks."

"Fine, Lord Whittles. Shall I include gloves and slippers, too? Let me guess—her feet are neither long nor short?"

Whatever response Charles provided Madame Starling, he could never recall. His daily allotment for decision-making had been exceeded. He quit the boutique, fetched Lightning from the stable, and returned to Canon Ashby. Rejoicing that it no longer rained, he also praised his Maker that he would never have to visit a modiste's shop again.

Within a short distance, he groaned and Lightning's ears pricked. As father, he would have a hand in preparing Arianna's come out in another thirteen years. If he and Winsome have other daughters, his fate seemed writ in stone. As that grim reminder struck him, it began to drizzle.

"Of all that's wonderful!"

His spirits buoyed, however. In thirteen years, Winsome would assist Arianna in selecting a debutante's wardrobe as she would for the subsequent daughters they'd have. As father, his involvement in the matter would be tangential, at best. His small task would be to pay the bills. He exhaled in relief.

Reaching inside his damp jacket, he touched the packet containing Winsome's engagement ring. He spurred Lightning into a canter, grinning as he rode back to Canon Ashby, despite the heavy rains.

Chapter 15

"Are you pleased with yourself or the dress?" Charles' dry humor resonated in his baritone voice as he applauded Winnie's pirouette.

Embarrassed to be caught twirling in the hall, Winnie pinched the soft new material of the dress Mrs. Reynolds had made her. "I think the village seamstress did a wonderful job, don't you? I love how soft this is."

"But brown? I asked you not to get such a dreary color."

"This is appropriate for my station, I'll have you know." She pressed her hand against the modest décolletage showing and admitted, "But depressing, for all that, I grant you."

"Winsome, you're my fiancée—a prospective bride and soon-to-be mother. If you doubt it, look at the ring on your third finger."

Winnie noted Bertram was present, which must be why Charles had pushed the façade, to make their betrothal appear genuine in front of an audience.

The countess didn't suspect, of course. As soon as Charles announced they were to wed, she insisted Winnie leave her room in the attic and occupy one of the guest chambers. It was a lovely set of rooms, with its own sitting area. She hoped the earl was as good at explaining the reasons for the fake betrothal as he had been inducing her to accept it. Winnie did not wish Lady Northampton to feel betrayed when she discovered their pretense, particularly when she'd been so kind.

"It *is* lovely." Gazing at the topaz ring, which twinkled up at her, she sighed. "I can't imagine why your mother didn't wear it. It's gorgeous. Thank you."

"Why would Mama wear it?" A puzzled expression coming over his face.

"Because it's so beautiful." She flexed her hand, admiring how the ring caught the light. The topaz dominated the setting and was surrounded by diamonds.

"It's an *engagement* ring."

"Yes, and I thank you for letting me wear it. It's very kind of you."

"I'm glad you enjoy it," he bit out.

Over the past week and more, they'd fallen into an agreeable routine. Charles accompanied her on long, morning strolls then she taught Arianna. She and Charles ate lunch together and answered correspondence. In the afternoons, Winnie assisted the countess while Charles gave Arianna riding lessons—or she gave her father giggling lessons, as the case may be. In the evenings, the entire Dryden family gathered for dinner and tea. Afterward she and Charles tucked Arianna into bed, wishing her 'goodnight' after listening to her prayers. Sometimes Charles read a bedtime story and Winnie sat quietly, listening. She'd been right to think he had a wonderful voice. Hearing the stories had been the loveliest part of her day.

It was the happiest time of her life since her mother's passing. She felt a strong sense of belonging here at Canon Ashby. Every once in a while, she'd catch Charles' gaze upon her and nearly convinced herself he regarded her with tenderness and affection.

Guarding her heart proved to be much more difficult than she originally thought. Charles insisted on treating her as a real fiancée, sneaking kisses and holding hands as they walked. This morning he'd pulled her into a dark stall of the stable, away from the grooms and kissed her senseless. Each time he pulled her toward him, she went without demur. It never occurred to Winnie to protest—she enjoyed his kisses far too much. She hadn't initiated anything, but when she saw that special light in his eyes—the signal that some loving was coming—pleasure warmed her.

Once she gained solitude, she wondered if she were becoming a light skirt. She looked forward to kissing Charles, but surely it was sinful to treat a phony fiancé as real?

151

Not once during their walks on the estate did Sir David show himself, but at odd moments, Winnie still experienced the troubling sensation of being watched. Inside Canon Ashby, so long as Charles was there, she felt safe. He'd already leveled the baronet with one glorious blow. If called upon to do it again, Winnie had no doubt he would.

Charles had been spot on when he predicted Sir David would spread rumors concerning them. Those tales didn't get much traction as Charles informed Vicar Turnbull they were engaged. That man, in turn, announced the happy news to the entire neighborhood.

"So, shall I ask Reverend Turnbull to have the banns read, Winsome?"

She nearly jumped from her skin. Placing her hand over her heart to settle its palpitations, she eyed Charles. His expression was so bland, so innocent, it was difficult to tell he was teasing her, but of course he was. She shook her head, dislodging that foolish hope he'd been serious. Not once in their time together had he mentioned deeper feelings for her. He was merely acting as her fake fiancé to protect her from her dastardly cousin, and helping himself to a handful of kisses as recompense.

"Ha, ha." She entered the library, tugging the lace cuffs of her new dress, enjoying the fashion splurge. "I'm a governess and nothing more. Not really. We know this betrothal is a pretense."

As Charles reached for the bell pull, his hand stayed. He then gave the rope a jerk and faced her.

"Pretense?" he asked, something in those eyes burned, but Winnie could not identify it.

"Yes," she said, rounding the desk and sitting at her usual place. She picked up the quill and sharpened it. "His lordship explained we could pretend to be betrothed while Sir David and Lady Broomstead remained at Landry House? He pointed out, his lordship, that is, that I'm better protected belonging to a herd than as a straggler. Safety in numbers and all that."

"What herd?"

"Not an actual herd. Just part of the Dryden family."

"My brother said that, did he?" he murmured, his voice flinty.

152

Bertram came to the open library door and Charles nodded to him and informed him they were prepared to have their luncheon provided.

"That explains the remark concerning Mama and the ring." He muttered, rubbing his forehead.

"I'm well aware you don't wish to marry me." She twirled the quill between her fingers, hoping she appeared nonchalant.

Leaning forward in his chair, he stabbed his finger in her direction, looking as if he would dispute that point until she said, "I thank you for protecting me, but I do hope the charade will end soon."

He sat back in his chair, his hand falling by the wayside. A moment of silence beat before she noticed a muscle throbbing along his jawline. His voice, when he next spoke, cut like a knife. "And why is that?"

His angry expression caught her off-guard. "Oh, I don't mean to offend you, Charles. After all, I'm grateful for your friendship."

"Grateful? Friendship?"

Scorn was packed into the two words and Winnie had no idea how to respond.

Bertram reappeared in the pregnant pause which followed, laden with a tray of sandwiches and a pitcher of lemonade. He removed the plates, napkins, and silverware before pouring the drink for Miss Montgomery.

Charles never touched the stuff.

The butler set a tankard of ale on the desk, closest to Charles. The poor man must have recognized the tension in the air for he made a quick, furtive move to scoot the ale further from the edge. Her lips twitched, remembering the culinary catastrophe Charles had set into motion her first evening here. Apparently, Bertram hadn't forgotten it, either.

"Leave us, please."

The butler obeyed, closing the library door, but not before Winnie glimpsed his grimace.

Rubbing the back of her neck, Winnie mumbled, "I just don't like Sir David's continued lurking."

"Nor I. Has he done anything more?" Charles' words were staccato-sharp.

"Nothing I can prove," she said, sagging into her chair.

"But?" He lifted an inquisitive eyebrow.

Pasting a false smile on her face, she injected all the cheerfulness she could muster into her voice. "Let's take up Parker's letter, shall we?"

"My dear." It sounded very much like a scold when he said the endearment like that. She was becoming accustomed to that blighting accent.

She scowled at the inkwell. "Sometimes I feel as if I'm being watched. Do you know the sensation? I despise it."

"Come to me immediately if you experience that again. Trust your instincts."

"Thank you."

The lines of Charles' face softened as their gazes met.

A pleasant lightness came over her, as if she existed at some midway point between heavenly sunshine and puffy, white clouds. Moments like this—and they were growing daily—cost her every ounce of self-respect to remember this was a phony engagement.

"You still don't trust me, do you?"

She watched his lips move, fascinated. It took a moment for his words to register, and she quickly shook her head. "I do."

"No, you don't. You believe I'm just as unreliable as your father or cousin." Anguish flitted across his features so rapidly, she wasn't certain if she had read it correctly.

"You're nothing like my father, Charles. You're very good with Arianna. You listen to her long-winded, long-winding tales as if she mattered. That's lovely to see."

"You're lovely."

She blinked. The quill snapped in half.

"Drat." She stared at the damage her hands wrought.

Charles rubbed his palms together, relishing her discomfort. "Later today new clothes will be delivered for you. You'll find a red ball gown I wish you to wear when you accompany me and my family to the Northampton Assembly

Monday next. You will be presented as my fiancée and shall be appropriately attired."

"Oh, but that's not nec—"

"Before you say something idiotish, I remind you that Mr. Turnbull has already informed the neighborhood of our betrothal. Sir David and Lady Broomstead remain at Mr. Landry's residence, so our charade must continue for now."

They stared at each other across the expanse of his desk. Despite her best efforts, the corners of her mouth twitched and the smile she didn't want to give made an appearance.

"Bertram!" he called, pulling the bell cord. Once the butler re-opened the door, Charles asked for him to bring a comb and pair of scissors.

"Yes, sir."

He stood and removed his jacket.

"What are you doing?"

Bertram returned and Charles indicated with a nod for the butler to hand the items to her. Winnie took the comb and scissors as Charles tucked a napkin into his collar.

"You're going to give me a haircut outside."

"With one hand?"

"Yes, Lord save me."

"But I rescinded that condition, remember?" She laughed.

"Come with me. I'm going to earn your trust if it's the last thing I do, Winsome Montgomery, even if that means giving you mine first."

"Charles."

He carried an occasional chair to the flagstone verandah, placed it in the sunshine then sat.

Charles really meant it! He was going to allow someone to brandish a blade inches from his face. Immediately humbled, she stood behind him, tucking the napkin fully beneath his collar. The ends curled in the slight breeze while a bumblebee buzzed near the roses lining the verandah.

His hands clamped onto his knees until his knuckles blanched.

Moved, Winnie approached, running one hand along his broad shoulder, as if smoothing out the linen. The ripple of muscles beneath her fingertips reminded her of his power and strength and lovely, lovely warmth. Of its own accord, her hand massaged those muscles, freeing some of the knots.

The scent of those roses wafted through the spring air, tickling her nose.

"Listen to the bees. Soak in the sunshine and smell the roses. Isn't that relaxing now?"

Charles didn't say anything, keeping his eyes shut, but she detected a slight uptick on the corners of his mouth. His knuckles were no longer whitened.

She tucked the comb and scissors into her sling and eased her arm out of it. With both of her hands free, she was able to run her fingers through his silky dark hair. Her arm was a little stiff, but she'd be a fool not to take advantage of this opportunity to the fullest extent. She tugged the ends of his hair at the nape, working her way over his scalp. Her fingertips pressed into tender skin, rubbing in small circles. She'd never done this for anyone. It felt unbelievably intimate, but so incredibly right, she didn't hesitate.

Tension left him the more she played with his collar-length hair.

"Mmm," he said. "That's nice."

A lump formed in her throat so that it would have been impossible to answer. Slowly, so as not to disturb him, she pulled the comb out of her sling and ran it through his hair. She walked around him in a leisurely fashion while his eyes remained closed. Free to study the handsome lines of his face, she watched in satisfaction as his expression relaxed.

The sounds of her breathing and his mixed with the faint buzzing from the bee. She said nothing, not confident her words would leave her throat without being choked out. She took a deep breath, smelling the roses and the masculine scent of Charles. At times she forgot to run the comb, so caught up in relishing the satiny feel of his hair against her palm.

His lips, tender and playful, now curved into a gentle smile. He'd become perfectly content, giving himself into her keeping. It was the highest compliment she'd ever received and she did not wish to ruin it. Mindful of that honor, she whispered a warning. "I'm going to start cutting now. How would you like it?"

"However you prefer."

Was that her imagination or did his voice seem lower?
"Very well."

She made the first cut at the back. "Oh dear."

"Winsome," he warned.

Giggling, she smacked his shoulder. "I'm only teasing. Besides, I'm sure I can even it up."

"Winsome!"

She ignored the mock-scold and said, "I'll hold the scissors so that the points will be toward the sky, away from you. All right?"

He nodded.

Slowly she snipped, using the fingers on her broken arm to rake through his hair and hold the strands. Mindful of his unease, she shuffled her feet, bit by bit, as she progressed around him. Quietude fell upon them. Invisible strands passed between her and Charles, weaving around them so that they were bound together in their own tiny sphere. The only sounds were the occasional rustle of her skirt, the *clip* of the scissors, and the bumble bee.

His eyes remained shut as she stood before him. Before she realized his intentions, he placed both of his hands on her hips and pulled her between his spread thighs. He wore a satisfied grin, but kept his eyes closed.

His heat surrounded her. In this position, her bosom was placed near his eye level. She wondered when he would peek. Would he be surprised at the view? Pleased? She was simultaneously mortified and thrilled Mrs. Reynolds had lowered the neckline. The expanse of skin she bared was modest, to be sure, but more daring that any of her own gowns, which buttoned up the neck.

She finished cutting his hair, but while his eyes remained shut, she figured he wouldn't know otherwise. So she opened the scissors and snapped them shut a few times, slicing aimlessly through air. It was deceptive and dishonorable, but Winnie was learning she was no better than she ought to be. She was a light skirt, at least where Charles was concerned. She might never have this chance again. She might never be so close to him. Was it wrong to savor this time? She'd worry about that later. For now there was just her and Charles and a lazy bee buzzing the outskirts of the verandah. She worked the scissors, taking her time, hoping he'd peek…

The grip at her waist tightened and Charles' breathe quickened. He'd looked.

Her scissors began to vibrate. She made several short snips, scolding herself for being so affected until she heard him grind his teeth. At least she wasn't the only one experiencing these lovely, warm, frustrating sensations.

"Are you all right, Charles?" She gathered her courage to look down at him.

"I'm fine," he croaked, his gaze trained on her bare neckline.

Her intake was audible, but she remained still, her bosom hovering near his gaze.

"You are lovely, my dear."

He looked in her eyes. His eyes had darkened and the grooves alongside his cheeks were pronounced in his somber expression.

She wet her lips and he moaned. A warm feeling blossomed in her lower belly and the pair of scissors clattered to the flagstones. Her hand slid around his neck and massaged his nape. He leaned forward, slowly and deliberately, giving her a chance to withdraw, but she didn't. She didn't know what he planned to do, but she very much wanted to find out.

He brought her closer. His mouth touched the sensitive skin above her bodice. She squeezed his shoulders, encouraging him. Reading her response correctly, Charles kissed the tops of her breasts. Delicious sparkles traveled up and down her body. His hand left her hip to cup her breast. The pad of his thumb passed over the material, caressing her nipple.

She felt its hardening, responding to the friction. It was heavenly, but not enough. She wasn't sure what she needed, she only knew a lack of something.

"Please, Charles," she whispered.

His fingers quickly delved beneath the lace-edged bodice until he plucked her breast from the material. He squeezed rhythmically, catching the nipple between his thumb and forefinger.

158

She swayed toward him. As if mesmerized, she watched Charles press his dark, shorn head into her proffered bosom. His fingers worked to unfasten the buttons on the front of her dress. The material was shoved to the sides so that his tongue could search over her breast. In long, slow passes he blazed the trail to her hardened nubs, attending one then moving toward the other.

Winnie clutched his head.

With quick, swirling moves of his clever tongue, he brought a nipple deep into his mouth and suckled. Her fingers rested along Charles' jawline, feeling its movements as his mouth worked on her delicate flesh, stoking the flames in her to a fevered-pitch. She squeezed her eyes shut, to better focus on the many new sensations which coursed through her. Tension invaded her body, making her feel like a coiled spring. So this was desire, this heat and wetness and leashed passion. She'd always enjoyed his kisses, but now knew the sensitivity of her breasts surpassed that of her lips.

"Oh, Charles. Charles, darling." She writhed on his lap, clutching him in a desperate bid to pull him closer. Overwhelmed, yet still not satisfied, she didn't know what she needed. Charles would know, though. He held the key to unlocking these mysteries.

"Darling! Wh—ow!"

A single, heavy blow struck her right shoulder blade, causing those lovely, warm, floating sensations to scatter.

"Bloody hell!"

Her fogged brain took its time to clear. Coming back to reality, she spied the scissors she'd earlier dropped to the flagstones. Beside them, a rock wobbled before losing its momentum and coming to a rest.

Charles stood her up and rose in one fluid movement. He yanked the front of her dress closed and re-buttoned it. Later she would cringe that he'd unbuttoned so many without her knowledge, but now it barely penetrated her thoughts.

"Are you hurt, Winsome?"

She nodded, unable to reach the bruise on her back and answered incongruously, "I don't think so."

Charles stalked to the edge of the verandah, spied the black dot of Sir David's head bobbing above the hedgerow surrounding the garden. "Damn him!"

Drained and shaky, Winnie stumbled across the threshold and slumped into the nearest library chair.

"Hello there! We need help here!" Charles hollered.

Within moments, Bertram appeared, his normal, impassive expression registering shock.

Charles dragged the butler to Winnie, who pressed her hand against her mouth. "Take care of Miss Montgomery. She's been struck by that rock." He crossed to the desk, opened a drawer, and withdrew a pistol.

"I-I-I-I," she stuttered, horrified as he loaded the gunpowder and prepared the flintlock. The glittering anger blazing in his eyes frightened her.

"What are you planning, Mr. Dryden?" Bertram asked, alarm written in his bulging eyes.

Charles strode to Winnie and kissed her forehead.

Jolted out of her shock, she gripped his forearm and begged, "No, Charles! Please don't go. He'll kill you! Leave it be."

"Put some ice on that bruise, dear. Bertram, call the physician to look after Winsome."

"Charles, no! No!" Her scream reverberated around the library, which suddenly felt empty without Charles in it.

Chapter 16

It was after midnight when Charles crept into his chamber at Canon Ashby. Dragging his body over the threshold, he ran a shaky hand through his shorn hair. Quietly, he set his pistol on the highboy dresser, crossed to his bed, and plopped down. A single brace of candles provided light in the room, but shadows crawled upon the rug, stretching across the floor he'd traversed. The shadows were sinister lengths, pulling evil from its base then casting it upon the earth.

"That bad?" Pursing his mouth, Spec stood, arms folded, in the doorway to the dressing room. "What do you mean being gone all evening? The women folk have been worried about you, but I convinced the countess and Miss Montgomery you slipped into Culworth for a pint of ale."

Startled, Charles looked at his valet. "No, more's the pity. I've spent the last several hours with the constable, ensuring that Sir David's locked up."

"Good, good. Hope the blighter gets transported for hurting Miss Montgomery like that."

With an air of preoccupation hanging over him, Charles made a half-laugh, rubbing the back of his neck. "Oh, no. He won't be transported."

Sensing the captain's tension, Spec quietly poured the warm buckets of water he'd set on the hearth into the bath. Then he helped an agitated captain remove his boots, peel off his breeches.

Charles sat in the tub, splashing water over his torso and head. He closed his eyes, wishing he could blot out what he'd seen.

When he opened his eyes, he found his alarmed valet staring at him.

Spec placed a towel on a nearby stool for his use. "What happened?"

His actions mechanical, Charles dipped his fingers into the jar of soap and scrubbed the scented concoction over his hair, arms, and chest. He was covered in trail dust, blood, and sweat. He needed to eradicate the stench of death, which clung to him like a thin layer of oil upon water. Charles ran a soapy washcloth over every part of his body, wiping off the traces of the horrible, ghastly day until he could feel clean, body and soul.

He leaned forward to allow Spec to wash his back.

"I found Sir David in the gardens, skulking about. He tethered his horse to the shepherd statute. I saw it and ran toward it, but he reached the bay first and mounted. He kicked my shoulder when I grabbed his stirrup then galloped away. Flynn brought Lightning around and I gave chase. We rode for miles— both horses were lathered."

"You didn't shoot?" Spec asked in incredulous tones.

"No, I didn't. He took me through back woods, down winding trails. Any shot I got off might have ricocheted or been inaccurate, but thank God I didn't shoot him. Otherwise, I might never have found the body."

"What body?"

"Lady Broomstead. He killed her."

"Good Lord."

"He'd taken her to Landry's gamekeeper's hut. Broke her neck. Buried her in a shallow grave."

"Good Lord," said the man of few correct words.

Charles stared into space while Spec cleared his throat a couple of times. It was a long while before either man registered the scratching at the chamber door. Spec, as if in a fog, walked over and cracked it open.

"Has Charles returned? Is he well?" Winnie's faint voice drifted to him.

Lunging for the towel, Charles rose swiftly, wrapping it around his waist as water dripped off him. "Winsome?"

Spec tugged her into the room, laying his forefinger against his lips. "Shh," he admonished her, although the warning was unnecessary.

Winsome Montgomery was speechless. Her eyes boggled upon seeing his naked body, but he noticed she didn't look away—at least, not immediately. She wore her thick flannel dressing gown and robe—the one he couldn't wait to burn—with its high necked frills.

"Where's your sling?" he asked.

"The doctor said I didn't need it any longer. My arm's healed."

The valet muttered something about joining Sally at the tavern and quietly let himself out of the room.

Charles's hand raised part-way to acknowledge Spec's departure before he lowered it, realizing his man had already left the room.

She stood just a little inside the door, clasping her hands as color rushed into her cheeks. Casting her gaze toward the floor, she murmured, "I thought I'd heard you return and just wanted to make sure you were…you were safe. I was worried, you see."

He stepped out of the tub and crossed the room to her. He gripped her shoulder with one hand as the other fastened onto his towel, anchoring it around his hips. "Are you hurt? Bruised?"

Her gaze lifted some, but remained fixed at his chest, rather than meeting his eyes. His grasp tightened. "Tell me, Winsome, did he hurt you?"

Finally he looked into a glorious pair of eyes. A sheen of tears made her topaz eyes gleam like the jewel he'd placed on her finger.

"A bruise on the left shoulder. It's nothing. I was so worried about you. I had to see for myself that you were all right." Her hand caressed his cheek and he nuzzled her palm.

She had a healing touch, something he desperately needed right now. The image of Lady Broomstead's lifeless body seared his brain. The poor woman died a violent death at the hands of her husband. No lady deserved such a fate. The temptation to wrap his arms around Winsome and simply hold her made him begin to shake with need. He needed to feel all those lovely curves of her

163

warm body, assure himself she was safe, that her cousin couldn't hurt Winnie as he had his wife.

"What is it, Charles? What happened?"

He shook his head. He did not wish to burden her with that tale. He stepped back to get some distance, gain a tighter grip on his raw emotions. He told himself that Winsome was fine. Sir David was bleeding and shackled in the tavern cellar, awaiting his hanging. There was no need for these waves of panic pulsing over him. If only he could believe it...

Belatedly remembering the improprieties, he said, "It's not proper for you to be here. You must leave. I'm trying to be honorable, Winsome, but now is not the time to test my limits."

"I don't wish to impose, I just needed to know you are well."

"I am." He flushed, detecting movement beneath the towel. Part of him was surprised he could 'rise' to the occasion after the grueling past few hours, while another part of him ruefully recognized the inevitability whenever he was near Winsome.

Quickly he scanned the room, grateful to find Spec had laid out his silk robe. "Turn around," he ordered, donning his robe before draping the towel around his neck.

"You are *not* well," she argued, choosing now of all times to be stubborn. "Something's wrong. I can tell. What is it?"

"For the love of God, Winsome, leave it be!"

"Leave it be? Leave it be?"

The sharpness of her tone let him know reprimanding her wasn't be a winning strategy.

She demanded, "Didn't I tell *you* that before you dashed out the library?"

He half-smiled, feeling some of the tension drain from his body as her indignation struck him as funny. Avoiding her gaze, he plopped down in his chair and rested his head against the back. In a lazy drawl, he said, "I beg your pardon, but it remains that you shouldn't be here. This puts you in a hopelessly compromising situation where you may be forced to accept me as your husband and not just as phony fiancé."

Silence reigned. He heard a rustle of skirts, a few clinks as she opened the glass decanter and poured the brandy. Another clink signaled she'd replaced the crystal stopper. He heard her approach, catching a scent of her fragrance as she drew near to the side of his chair. Charles cracked an eyelid.

"Is that for me, my dear?"

"For you." She handed him the glass.

He murmured, "Will wonders never cease? And here I thought you disapproved of my drinking."

"Only to the point of drunkenness."

He raised his glass in a salute. "Touché."

She gave a small smile. "I thought you could use a strong belt."

Taking a long, slow swallow, Charles heaved a sigh of contentment. "I did. Thank you." His head fell back and he closed his eyes, making an effort to regulate his breathing. She stood nearby quietly but with an air of expectation. He knew she was waiting for him to explain the day's events, but he didn't wish to at that moment. All Charles wanted was sleep. Nice, restorative sleep. Well, that wasn't entirely true. What he really wanted was a vigorous tumble in bed. He'd like nothing better than to tup Winsome, slide his shaft into her warm depths and seek the oblivion he knew he'd find in lovemaking.

"Now run along to your room. You've seen that I'm well and you may return to your bed and sleep soundly. We can talk about the rest in the morning."

Time passed. She hadn't moved away, nor had she said anything. Suspicious, he lifted his head to glare at her, but she wasn't looking at him. She remained rooted to the spot, staring at the Gainsborough above his mantel. The intense longing in her expression sent a shaft of concern through him.

"Winsome? What is it, dear?"

"Did you win this playing cards?" Her voice throbbed with emotion as she pointed to the painting.

Mystified, he slowly admitted, "Yes. I gave it to Vivian—she liked it. It was in the drawing room at Kedington, but I brought it here with me, not knowing how long Arianna and I would reside here. I won it playing whist…"

The pieces fell into place. The earlier conversations about her father gambling away their once-prosperous estate, how he'd cheated her of her dowry…

"That was your father?"

Nodding, she choked out, "My father lost it playing whist with a soldier shortly after Mama died."

"Me. I was the soldier."

"Yes, you." She pointed to the figure in the red gown, the only pop of color in the drab foreground. "The woman in the meadow was my grandmother."

Her eyes were shining, glowing with…pride? Joy? Relief? He couldn't tell.

He took her hand and gave it a reassuring pat. "Of course you may have it back, Winsome. Your father should never have wagered it."

"No."

He nodded, thinking she agreed with him until she said, "No, Sir Vernon ought not to have wagered it, but I'm so glad he did."

"What's that?"

Her eyes gleamed with a mischievous light.

He barely had time to acknowledge it before she crawled onto his lap, wrapped her arms around his neck, and kissed his throat. Stunned, he remained still, wondering what her intentions were. Did she know how this flirtation would end? Did she have any idea what she was risking by touching him like this?

Her hand roamed over his chest and his arms locked about her, securing her. He could feel her lips curve into a smile as she pressed sweet kisses along his jawline then nipped his earlobe. Slowly, he began to comprehend that she knew precisely what she was doing and where this was leading. Pleased, but puzzled, he turned his head so that their mouths would meet. And then he forgot about everything except loving Winsome.

Her tongue licked the seam of his lips and then invaded his mouth in the way he'd taught her. He soon took control, holding her cheeks as they fed kisses to each other. He was hungry for her, ravenous. She denied him nothing, matching his need until he felt as if flames engulfed him.

166

So much for trying to regulate his breathing. His breath hitched when her hand snuck inside his robe. She flattened her palm over his heart, grazing the nipple and causing another sharp intake.

"Winsome," he groaned. His hands smoothed over her, molding the luscious curves of her body, re-mapping her body anew. He reveled in her warmth, in the dips and swells of her. The world faded away as they explored one another. Caught up in the silky slide of her tongue and the softness of her body, his desire spiraled. She squirmed, causing her bottom to move against his erection. He had to suck in a cooling breath of air. When she repeated the act, he became convinced she'd done it intentionally and his temperature spiked.

"Charles."

The breathlessness in her voice pierced him. Listening to her soft murmurings of passion caused thrills to ripple beneath his skin. Whatever qualms he'd had about this late night tryst struggled to the surface of his mind. Gripping her tightly, he stood up and carried her to the bed.

"I want to love you, here and now. If you won't belong to me forever, you'd better go while you can. This is your only chance."

Her shiny eyes and bright smile caught him off-guard. "I belong with you, Charles."

Still he hesitated, not quite in command of himself nor sure of her. He set her down on her feet, bracing her shoulders as he tried to impress upon her the seriousness of the step they were about to take. "Once we make love, we will be married, Winsome, as soon as I can arrange it. You understand this? This is no fake betrothal. It becomes real."

Slowly a dazzling smile burst forth. She snagged the ends of his belt and worked the knot loose. She spread the lapels, stepped into his arms, and pressed herself against him.

"I understand. I trust you." Her head dipped so that her tongue could trace his collarbone.

With a deep-throated moan, he rolled his shoulders, shrugging off his robe.

He watched her looking at him in his full glory, nothing hidden. When she blushed and turned away to climb against the headboard, the adorable shyness of that tugged his heartstrings. She was so vulnerable, so innocent.

"Comfy?"

Giving him a wobbly smile, she nodded. "Shall I…shall I remove my robe and gown?"

"Most certainly." He climbed onto the bed, sitting on his haunches as he awaited the unveiling.

Her hands shook slightly as she untied the ugly flannel robe. She lifted her bottom and whipped it away from her body, tossing it to the floor. Her eyebrow arched, as if questioning the need to remove her gown, as well, but he remained quiet, allowing her to choose whatever was most comfortable for her.

"Ehem." She unfastened the long row of buttons, and to his everlasting gratitude, the edges of the bodice drooped, allowing a healthy show of bosom. An odd light, almost feverish, came into her eyes. Winsome sat forward, tucking her knees beneath her. Then she unbuttoned her cuffs.

He groaned. Would there never be an end to the torment? Half of England's buttons must be sewn onto her blasted gown!

She tried to lift her hem, but the material was trapped beneath her legs. She tugged, but it failed to come free.

"I don't wish to rip it," she mumbled, embarrassment staining her cheeks.

Egads! Even when she was clumsy, she was adorable.

"Stand up," he croaked, extending his hand to assist.

Winsome stood on the bed, her feet sinking into the soft mattress. She placed both of her hands on his shoulders to maintain her balance.

Ducking beneath her gown, Charles was surrounded by the soft, white muslin and faced a pair of satiny thighs. He ran his hands along her calves, studying the shape of her legs. Bending ever so slightly, he pressed his lips to the side of her knee and felt her start.

"Charles."

Her hand cupped the back of his head through the muslin. "Charles," she groaned again.

"Lean on me, if you must, Winsome, but don't let your knees buckle, for God's sake."

Once more his hands coasted along her legs, traveling upward over smooth inner thighs. He inhaled the scent of her, using his fingers to part the curls at the juncture of her legs.

"You're so lovely."

She swayed, stumbled then righted herself.

Proud of her for remaining upright, his fingers stroked the folds, relishing their damp state. His hand traced her core, rubbing a syncopated rhythm. When her flesh began to weep, he inserted one finger inside her, feeling her muscles clamp down on his digit. He moaned in pleasure. He continued to play, teasing her. He added another finger, working to widen her channel, pleased when her body accommodated him.

"Charles," she gasped. "What are you…doing?"

"Pleasuring you, I hope, my love."

"Whatever you're doing, don't stop," she panted.

He felt the unmistakable tightening of her inner muscles and heard her gasping. Between her moans and the tightening grip on the back of his head, Winsome was on the brink of her first sexual experience.

"Let go, Winsome. Let it happen."

"I…I don't know—" Her legs started shaking and she bucked, bringing her hips into his face.

Charles groaned. He knew exactly the temptation that posed, but mindful of the newness of this experience, he denied himself that pleasure. He didn't want to go too fast for her and risk shocking her. Silently promising there'd be other opportunities to please her that way, he placed one hand on her buttocks and one at her back so that he could lower her to the bed. He stretched out alongside her, grabbed her gown's hem, and lifted it to her belly.

"What was that?" she whispered.

"Pleasure. Men and women find it different ways."

"How do you find it?"

"Whenever you touch me…"

She turned to face him. Her palms rolled over his scalp. "Like this?"

Charles inwardly groaned. "Yes, that's nice, but this..." He took her hand and brought it to his erection, sliding against her palm. She gripped him and he sucked in some air, unsure if he'd last much longer. It had been too long and he wanted her so much. "But that's...so intense."

She ran her hands over his cock, staring and marveling at it. "It feels nice."

His shuddered laugh followed. "You're the master of the understatement. May I?"

At her nod, he removed the gown and cast it aside. It met the same fate as her robe. Drinking in the sight of his Winsome, fully naked, he felt himself harden even more. He hadn't thought it possible. She possessed a pair of slim ankles which led to a set of calves that were slightly curved. Her thighs were lean and strong. Her hips flared out over a flat stomach. Above the slender waist rose two mounds of rose-tipped breasts, soft and round and perfect.

"You're so beautiful."

"You, too."

His lips pressed against the valley between her breasts and followed a trail to her flat stomach. Her legs slithered across the bedcover, restless. So his hand sought the apex of her legs, working in the damp crevices to prepare her for his entry. It wouldn't be long. He'd never wanted a woman as much. Sheathing himself in her was all he could think about. He craved that feeling of being cocooned, cradled between her thighs.

"This may hurt, darling, although I hope not too badly," he cautioned as he moved over her. He placed the tip of his cock at her entrance, shaking with the effort to restrain his desire.

"I love you, Charles." She clutched his shoulders, her fierce whisper touching a place deep inside him, a place he'd forgotten he had.

He drove into her, breaking through her barrier then halted. He willed himself not to move until her body adjusted to him.

Her hands fluttered above his shoulders and he kissed her mouth then murmured nonsensical words, promising her everything would be all right.

She sighed then worked her fingers through his hair. It was the signal he needed to proceed.

"Winsome," he breathed as he began to move in her. He closed his eyes, luxuriating in the feel and fragrance of her, in her warm softness. She was the ocean and he wanted to drown in her depths. This is where he belonged. Charles didn't know where he ended and she began. "I love you."

Chapter 17

Something warm and hairy rested upon her waist and after a brief moment of panic, Winnie grinned, remembering. Turning her head very slowly, so as not to disturb him, she peered through the darkness, studying Charles' face. Her hand glanced off his brow in a caress. Slowly, his lashes lifted. She watched as his eyes registered blank comprehension then turned to wonder. He smiled, drawing her closer then kissed her cheek.

"That was wonderful."

"Yes, it was," he replied, nuzzling the side of her throat.

"Is it always that way?"

He pulled back. "I won't hurt you again, if that's what you're asking."

"No." She lightly tapped his broad shoulders, the ones she'd admired since first seeing him at Bannock's Inn. "I meant…is it always like that? So shatteringly delicious."

"No, Winsome. It's never been like that for me until you."

She didn't even try to hide the pleasure his statement gave her. Wrapping her leg around his, she picked up his hand and played with the long fingers of his own. Those were marvelous instruments. Oh, the things his touch had done to her. He'd introduced her to passion, taking and giving with his innate generosity.

How remarkable that her father's dereliction and betrayal had formed links in the chain of events which led her to him. If Sir Vernon hadn't gambled the Gainsborough, Charles wouldn't have sent along twenty-five pounds. If her father spent more time at home in his library, he would have remembered Charles' letter,

172

found the money and spent it, thereby preventing Winnie from using it to escape Stanhope and travel to London. Although she hadn't known it at the time, she had benefited from Charles' largess. Even when he made such a horrid impression upon her at Bannock's Inn.

He kissed the top of her hair. "Why do you smell like the verandah garden?"

Smiling again, she said, "I mix rose petals in my rinse."

"I love it." He squeezed her tight. "I love everything about you."

They cuddled like that beneath the covers, wrapped in each other until finally her curiosity raised its head and sniffed the air. "Charles, what happened to Sir David?"

The earlier warmth vanished as Charles withdrew and rose from the bed. He padded across the carpeted floor, picked up his robe, and put it on. He stood before the darkened window, peering into a murky landscape as he ran his hand over the crown of his head.

"Charles?"

"He's been taken into custody and awaits trial. He committed a hanging offense."

"He did? What did he do?"

Slowly, he turned around, watching the effect his words had upon her. "He killed his wife."

"What?"

He nodded.

"Gwyn's dead? Why? How?" Her palms splayed as she repeated, "Why?"

Charles went to the brandy decanter, splashed the liquor into a glass then returned to the bed, thrusting it toward her. "Here. Drink this."

Too shocked to object, Winnie took his advice. After she'd swallowed a sip, he frowned then brought the glass to her mouth again, indicating she should drink more. Once she consumed the brandy, he spoke.

"I chased him to the gamekeeper's hut on Landry's estate. He cursed me. Fellow was very annoyed to have seen us on the verandah with my mouth on…well, when I kissed you."

173

Winnie shook her head. "I still can't believe I allowed such liberties."

"Yes, well, thank you." He smiled briefly.

"And then what happened?"

"Sir David rode to the back of the hut and dismounted. By happenstance, he dismounted near a shovel and picked it up. I think he intended to use it to bludgeon me."

"Oh no!"

"Not to worry, dear. At that moment, Landry and two other gentlemen emerged from the hut. They'd been searching for Lady Broomstead, who'd gone missing that morning. Of course, once they appeared, the baronet's attitude completely altered. He became charming, affable, tried to usher us back into the building. When Landry mentioned his wife had gone missing, Sir David shrugged it off, saying something along the lines that she'd no doubt turn up."

"Odd."

"Yes, well, I picked up the shovel, thinking to return it to outbuilding for the gamekeeper, but I stumbled over a tree root— what I thought was a tree root, and dropped it. When I reached down, I saw it."

She waited, watching Charles swallow. He massaged a knot in his throat, as if it were blocking his speech.

"It wasn't a tree root I tripped on, Winsome." Threads of time spun out several beats before he said, "It was the toe of her boot. He'd buried her in a shallow grave behind the hut."

Words refused to form in her mind.

Charles' face was a picture of anguish.

Without speaking, she rose from the bed and hugged him tightly, rubbing small circles of comfort onto his back. He clutched her so hard, it hurt, but she ignored her discomfort, concerned only with removing that haunted look. What a grisly discovery to make. Winnie took a shuddering breath, swallowing bile.

"What's been done to him?"

"We bundled him up and hauled him to Culworth. He's being held in the cellar, awaiting trial."

"Will he hang?"

"Yes."

"Oh, Charles." She kissed him again, bestowing tokens to assuage his pain. At first he frowned, lost in the sour recollections, but eventually his scowl lessened and he began to kiss her back.

Holding his hand, Winnie returned to the bed, bringing his body down with hers amongst the pillows. In the dark hours before dawn, they made sweet love again. She whispered words of love and he answered in that low, thrilling voice of his. When her sounds of passion increased in volume, he kissed her again, muffling the noise, but she felt his smile as he did so. The cares of the world were forgotten as they loved each other.

Later, after Charles fell asleep, she slid off the mattress as surreptitiously as she could. She donned her gown and robe, and eased the door open. Peering down the hallway, she slipped out of the chambers and returned to her room, undetected. Going about her daily ablutions, she couldn't help by marvel at the unfamiliar twinges in her body. She'd never known passion and had no idea the joy in giving pleasure to another.

To think she would have that magnificent body of Charles at her disposal for the rest of her life!

She had to splash cold water on her face to cool her excitement. She returned to her bed, hating it immediately. It was cold and empty, but she slept for a couple of hours. When she awoke, she dressed in her new round gown made of wool then donned coordinating slippers Madame Starling sent. She adored this lilac outfit. A chain of daisies had been stitched near the hemline. Never before had she owned a dress of this color. Looking at her reflection in the window, she nodded, pleased with how well it suited her coloring. Charles had been correct about Madame Starling. She was a wiz with needle and thread. In her excitement, she nearly skipped to Arianna's room.

"Wake up, my dear Arianna," Winnie sing-song to the sleepyhead.

"No," she mumbled, burying her face deeper into her pillow.

"You must. It's a glorious day and you wouldn't wish to miss it, would you?"

Another grumbling from the tiny person in bed suggested that Winnie over-rated the value of sunshine. After a little more

175

coaxing, Arianna's chubby fists rubbed sleep from her eyes. Blinking herself awake, her mouth took the shape of an 'O.'

"How pretty, Miss Monty! This is a new gown?" She touched the flowers embroidered above the hem.

"Yes. Isn't it pretty? This color is called lilac and those are daisies. What would you like to wear today?"

She thought about it a good long while. "I have something like this…" Arianna hopped off her bed and dug through her chest of drawers, rustling tissue paper which Juju laid over each dress.

"The lavender one?"

"Yes. Lafflinder."

"Fine," said Winnie, her heart swelling.

By marrying Charles she would have not only his handsome, strong, virile body, but his delightful little girl. Winnie would never be lonely again. Their family was going to be such a happy one!

As she helped Arianna into her gown, she insisted the girl don her pinafore, meeting unusual resistance to the idea. Winnie explained, "You don't wish to dirty your dress."

"But I don't like my pinafore!" Arianna whined.

"What's this?"

"It's plain and boring. And I hate it!"

Winnie clucked her tongue. "Hate is such a strong word, child. Please don't use it."

Reluctantly, Arianna begged her pardon.

Squatted down to be on her eye level, Winnie asked, "Why do you say the pinafore is plain?"

With tears in her eyes, Arianna pointed to Winnie's embroidered hem. "It doesn't have the flowers like your skirt does."

Her lips twitching in amusement, she managed to sound somber as she said, "And we want our gowns to match, don't we? Well, I'll have to embroider flowers onto your pinafore."

"Oh, please. Maybe a row of lafflinder daisies?"

Too wise to argue there was no such thing, Winnie merely nodded and promised, "Let's do so after lessons. You'll need to wear this for breakfast, though."

"That's all right and tight then." Arianna's clear voice rang out like a bell as, hand-in-hand, she skipped to the nursery to meet Juju.

Alone, Winnie entered the breakfast room, which the countess had renewed with a fresh coat of cream paint. The curtains were made of red toile, and the chairs covered with pink and cream stripes upholstery. The earl was already breaking his fast and it appeared Charles had finished his meal and remained to sip his coffee. He was wearing his traveling clothes. Upon spying her hovering in the doorway, Charles smiled and stood. He took her hands then pecked her cheek in a husbandly manner.

"Good morning! How are you today?"

Winnie tried to keep her cheeks from over-heating and utterly failed. Glancing at the table, she murmured a greeting to the earl.

Lord Northampton's gaze swiveled from her to his brother then back again to her. He made a deep chuckle. "Good morning, Miss Montgomery. What are your plans for the day?"

"Well, since it's promising to be so nice outside, I thought to take Arianna to the gardens. She wishes to learn embroidery. Are you going somewhere, Charles?"

"Yes, to London," he said. "For the special license to marry. I should be back on Thursday or Friday at the latest, if the road conditions are tolerable."

"Oh. When would you like the ceremony?"

"Thursday or Friday," he quipped. "As soon as I return."

Winnie grinned, shaking her head at her fiancé's impudence.

"On the front steps of Canon Ashby, if I don't mistake the matter," Lord Northampton said drily.

Charles nodded, grinning from ear to ear.

"For a man who didn't wish to re-marry, you appear remarkably pleased with yourself. Just remember, little brother, that you owe your future happiness to me," said the earl.

"Naturally." Charles looked at her. "You understand we must defer to the head of the Dryden family."

"Naturally," she mimicked to shared laughter.

Lord Northampton pointed out, "While you're in London, you should insert a notice in the papers."

"Yes," Charles agreed.

"While you're at it," Lord Northampton continued, "why don't you advertise for the new employees you'll need at Kedington? You'll want to hire them now so that they'll have sufficient time to prepare the house while you and Miss Montgomery take a bridal trip."

"Is this right, Charles? Do you plan to hire servants for Kedington?"

"Yes. Spec and I hired a couple to maintain the house. The wife cooks while the husband is the steward. Obviously, we'll require more servants."

"Stanhope's butler and housekeeper, the Dobsons, are seeking new employment. They're like family to me—"

"Say no more, Winsome." Charles laughed, flinging up his palm. "Write them a letter and direct them to Kedington. Inform them to begin service at the time of their choosing. I'll pay them the going rate. Either you or Mrs. Dobson can hire the other servants from the local community, however you prefer."

The smile broadened on her face. "Thank you, Charles."

"About that bridal trip, though…"

Winnie blushed.

"I don't wish to start off our marriage crossways, but I've already missed so much time with Ari—"

"I understand perfectly. We're a family, you, me, and Arianna. I can't wait to start our life together at Kedington. There's no need for a honeymoon."

"Do you mean that?" Charles rose and walked around the table to her.

"Yes."

Charles kissed her cheek then excused himself, saying, "I'm off to talk with Arianna about our marrying."

Winnie bit her lip. "Oh, I hope it doesn't upset her."

"Why should it?"

"Daughters are very possessive of their papas."

Northampton *tsked*. "I think my niece will be delighted to see her Miss Monty leg-shackled to her papa. Go on now, Charles."

When Winnie next saw her fiancé, he stood on the gravel drive outside Canon Ashby. She joined Lord and Lady Northampton to wish the travelers well on their journey. Spec was securing a travel bag to Lightning's saddle while Charles and Arianna looked on. When Charles spied Winnie, he squeezed his daughter's hand then jerked his head in Winnie's direction.

"Ooh, Miss Monty!" She squealed, bowling across the drive until she flung herself in Winnie's arms. "Papa told me you're going to be my new mama!"

"Yes." Her heart as full as her arms, Winnie hugged Arianna.

"All is well," Charles announced, making no effort to hide his satisfaction. He came up and wound his arms around the pair. He whispered into Winnie's ear, "The little minx said she always knew I liked you in that way."

Winnie giggled. "She did?"

"She did." He then kissed her, full on the mouth in front of his family and valet.

Heavens!

He waggled his dark eyebrows at her and she was struck again by how handsome he was, especially with his hair cut shorter.

"Be safe," she called after him once she thought it safe enough to use her voice again.

Charles leapt into the saddle then gave a jaunty salute.

She and Arianna waved until the pair were out of sight.

***

Sitting near the roses on the verandah, she had stitched two daisy petals into Arianna's pinafore before she noticed the girl was asleep. She never failed to amaze Winnie how she could be so chatty one minute then sound asleep the next. Winnie stood, stretched, and rolled her shoulders. One remained stiff and bruised from yesterday's pelting. Winnie considered whether she should carry the girl upstairs to her room then decided against it. Her shoulder was too sore to make the distance. Besides, there were plenty of footmen at Canon Ashby capable of lifting Arianna.

Winnie placed the threads and pinafore to the side then went inside to fetch one.

A few minutes later, she returned with James, but could find no trace of Arianna.

"She must have awaken when I came to get you," she apologized.

The footman asked, "Shall I check whether she's gone to her room?"

"Yes, please. I'll pop in to look at the kitchens. She's probably visiting Mrs. Halstead, begging for a strawberry tart."

The cook hadn't seen the girl so Winnie traced her steps back, rendezvousing with the footman in the library. He'd had no luck in searching the upstairs, either.

"Where could she be?" She glanced toward the verandah, spying a slip of paper speared onto a branch of the rose bush. A chill passed through her as Winnie snatched the paper and read, "Meet me at the pond. Come alone."

The footman followed her through the library onto the verandah. "What's the idea here? Oh, I say, Miss Montgomery, are you all right?"

She shook off the debilitating spell of dizziness which nearly overwhelmed her. In a croaky voice, she ordered, "Get me a pistol. Load it then fetch Flynn and Jeb from the stables. Tell them to bring their rifles. I'll meet you there."

The blond servant stood and stared, mouth agape. "Miss Montgomery? Why do you need a pistol?"

"I don't have time to explain—just do as I say. Now!"

Without waiting to see if James followed her instruction, Winnie dashed to her room, removing her useless slippers as she ran upstairs. Once there she rammed her feet into her half-jean boots then ran out the house and to the cobblestone yard.

James, the footman, met her with a pair of dueling pistols. He handed one to her, "Primed and ready."

She reached for the other and he drew it back, declaring, "This one's for me."

"Can you shoot?"

"We'll find out," he said grimly.

Rolling her eyes, she turned to Flynn and Jeb, the groomsmen. Rupert sauntered up, starting when he saw she held a pistol.

"Miss Monty!" he gasped.

"Arianna's been kidnapped by Sir David. He murdered his wife yesterday."

"What?"

Flynn and Jeb overheard and immediately began swearing.

"What do you want me to do, Miss Monty?" Rupert asked.

"You and James get to the fairies pond undetected. Stay hidden in the long grass."

"Jeb, mount up and ride to Mr. Landry's. See if he's taken her to the gamekeeper's hut. I have reason to think he might. If you see Sir David, shoot, but only if Arianna's safely out of the way. Now let's go."

Flynn blinked. The Scot shook his head, as if clearing out the cobwebs. "Are ye sure we shouldn't be tellin' his lordship? Methinks he may just have a say in—"

Winnie pivoted and marched toward the fairies pond, casting this taunt over her shoulder, "Tell him if you like. I haven't time. My cousin's a monster and I'm sure Arianna's frightened to death."

Propelled by anger and fear, Winnie covered the distance from the stables to the pond with speed. Jeb mounted a horse and took off toward Landry's estate and the gamekeeper's hut. James, Flynn, and Rupert followed Winnie to the pond. Rupert carried his blunderbuss, nestled between his shoulder blades with the strap across his torso. Flynn wore his belt and dirk. Winnie approached the pond as quietly as she could, praying to find Arianna. She snuck up on tip-toe and pressed against the hawthorn tree, using it as a shield.

She scanned Pan's territory.

Nothing.

That blighter had lured her on a wild goose chase. He must have taken her in the opposite direction, to the gamekeeper's hut on Landry's estate. Her insides felt heavy, weighed down by disappointment, until she rallied and remembered she'd sent their best shot, Jeb, to that location.

181

She and the others ran across Northampton's lands, yelling for Arianna.

Her legs burned from the unusual exercise. Winnie's side had a stitch in it, but she shoved the pain aside. She spotted a fleeting glimpse of something lavender ahead.

"Arianna! We're coming!"

James and Rupert outpaced her. The lad's blunderbuss bounced across his back. Flynn fell behind Winnie, unsheathing his Scottish dirk. James vaulted over the fence, swinging his legs to the side. Winnie didn't think she could accomplish that move so she ran to the stile and took the steps by two. She made a wobbly landing then lost her balance.

"Well done, lass!" Flynn grabbed her elbow and pulled her upward, dragging her until she found her footing.

Puffing and sweating, the pair closed the distance to the hut. The foursome were running all out. She spared a glance at James, glad the footman was fit, but unsure if he could shoot a moving target. Flynn's cheeks were flushed with exertion. His husky build was designed for strength, not speed. Still, if Sir David wished to brawl against the Scot, Winnie would let him. Rupert was probably the best shot of them—he'd been trained by Jeb, but Lord, she didn't want the lad to kill Sir David.

Winnie's heart thumped loudly and violently. Every prayer she knew vanished from memory so that all she could say was *keep her safe, dear Lord.*

They ran across a recently tilled field, in between the rows to avoid turning their ankles.

James hollered out, "You there! Stop!"

Sir David had flung Arianna over his shoulder as he jogged. For an instant, he slowed upon hearing the footman then picked up speed.

He was heading toward the gamekeeper's hut!

Ominous, it stood at the edge of the field.

Arianna's arms stretched toward Winnie as she wailed, "Miss Monty! Miss Monty!"

Winnie hid the pistol behind her back.

Her cousin spun upon hearing her name.

Winnie's chest heaved as she faced Sir David. "Put her down, David!"

Rupert removed his strap and brought the weapon up, bracing the blunderbuss against his shoulder, taking aim.

"No!" Winnie clutched his sleeve. "Arianna."

"Aye," he said, never lowering his weapon, but removing his finger from the trigger.

"Let her go." Winnie walked toward him, ignoring her heart thudding. The pistol felt heavy in her palm, but she clamped it against her thigh, hoping the fullness of her skirts hid it from view. "You want me, not her. I'll come with you if you let her go."

"You're outnumbered, lad," Flynn called, his Scottish brogue very pronounced. "Hand the lassie over."

Sir David's shirt was dirtied, the sleeves torn. A cuff dangled by a loose thread. He'd left his jacket behind somewhere, his pantaloons were stained. His nose was swollen and a line of dried blood stretched from the corner of his mouth down his neck. Charles hadn't told the whole story of how her cousin was taken into custody last night.

He shifted, holding Adrianna in place while he adjusted her weight. His splayed palm pressed against her back.

"Stop right there, mister," Rupert said.

David chuckled at the sight of the stable boy levelling his blunderbuss at him. "Trot along home, boy."

"Only if I take the girl with me."

James raised the pistol. "That goes double here."

"It's over, David." Winnie spoke calmly, widening her stance.

"Tell them to back off, Winnie."

She stayed silent.

"Tell them to drop their weapons. Don't anger me, Winnie." His hand curled into a claw, moving toward Arianna's thin neck.

"Don't hurt her! Lower your guns!"

"Yer a sick rot dastard!" Flynn, to the right of her, fumed, but he tossed his dirk into the ground, its hilt showing. James and Rupert threw down their weapons.

Where's Jeb?

183

She saw a gun barrel peek through opening in the cabin's doorway.

Good. I'll draw him into the hut.

"Release her and I'll come with you." Winnie tried to keep her voice even.

"Don't fancy an audience, cousin."

"No. Nor do I." Winnie took another step toward him. "Give them the girl. They'll take her home and we'll be together."

"That's all I ever wanted."

"I know." She nodded, trying to make her voice sound soothing.

Sir David set Arianna onto the ground.

"Go to Flynn, dear," Winnie told the girl who remained frozen in place. "Now, Arianna."

She squirmed and whimpered.

David gripped Arianna by her sash.

As if pushed, the girl lurched forward and landed face-down in the dirt.

Winnie heard the material rip, raised her pistol, and fired high.

Sir David reeled then clutched his shoulder. A stream of blood spurt between his fingers. "Bitch!"

James swooped in, grabbed Arianna on a dead run, and took off with her in his arms.

Rupert lunged for his firearm.

David lunged for her.

His face contorted in rage, he struck her head. Winnie cried out, her ears ringing from the backhanded blow. Landing hard in the dirt, she watched the sideways view of the Scot tackling her cousin and the departing form of James carrying Arianna. The edges of her vision blurred, but she smiled as fog closed in on the pair. A blissful muffling made Sir David's shouts incomprehensible. Noises sounded faraway, muted by a persistent ringing until even that was silenced. The world grew dim as Winnie slipped away.

Chapter 18

Never had Charles been more grateful for Lightning's speed and stamina, nor his valet and his steed, Buttercup. Ever since learning at Culworth that Sir David had escaped, he and Spec hightailed it back to Canon Ashby. He brought his gelding to a halt outside the front steps of Canon Ashby and vaulted onto the gravel drive. He threw the reins at Spec, which the former batman deftly caught.

"Give him a good rub down, won't you, Spec?"

"Aye, captain. Been thinking, though. If I were that baronet, I'd probably make for Dover or Plymouth. Board a ship. Sail to the Orient or such."

Charles nodded, feeling relief. "Excellent notion. Rather than face the hanging he deserves, I imagine the cowardly Sir David would bolt. If that's the case, then I'll apologize to you for over-reacting."

His valet chuckled. "You're as protective as a mother hen with those two females, your baby chicks. Face it, captain, you're in the petticoat line now."

Figuring he'd earned the ribbing, Charles didn't object. The grin on his face would have rendered any denial useless, anyway. It was true when they'd heard about Sir David's jail break, Charles experienced real terror. All that mattered was making certain Winsome was safe from her cousin. On the return trip home he'd tried telling himself that he was panicking. He would arrive home and find all was well.

"Mr. Dryden!" Bertram exclaimed upon seeing him enter the front door.

"Hello, Bertram. I…um…forgot something. Where's Miss Montgomery?" He strove to keep his inquiry bland, hoping the butler would overlook his tiny fabrication.

"Miss Montgomery?" The butler shook his head, regaining his usual impassivity. "Why, I'm quite sure I don't know, sir. Shall I inquire?"

He frowned. "Yes, please and be quick about it, man."

Bertram's brows raised a fraction, but his steps sped up, which was all that concerned Charles for the time being.

His instincts told him something was off, despite his rational brain arguing otherwise. When he heard heavy boots strike the oak planks, he whirled, fists clenched. Bursting through the connecting door to the kitchens, Spec panted, "Ain't nobody in the stables, captain."

Flabbergasted, Charles mumbled, "Devil it, why would the groomsmen abandon their posts?"

The knots in his stomach tightened. This was bad—whatever this was.

"Sure I don't know, but Flynn, Jeb, and the freckled boy—what's his name?"

"Rupert," he supplied.

"They're all gone, captain."

His mother glided into the foyer, blinking her surprise. "Charles, what on heavens are you doing back?"

"Do you know where Winsome is?"

She appeared taken about by his fierce tone. "I don't know, dear. The last time I saw her she and Arianna were in the garden, practicing their embroidery. Will, darling, Charles has returned to inquire into his fiancée's whereabouts."

"What's all the hullabaloo, Chas?" His brother stepped around their mother to clap Charles' shoulder.

"Sir David's escaped."

The news hit the earl with the same force it had struck Charles. That shared experience was hardly reassuring. His stomach began to churn, as it always had in the minutes leading up to battle. Preludes were the worst part of war.

Juju shouted from the top of the stairs, "Master Charles! Master Will! I can't find Arianna!"

Fear clutched his heart and gripped it in a new tighter, fiercer hold. Nothing in Wellington's army had prepared him for this.

"Bertram, outfit every male servant with ammo and weapon." Will barked to the butler then he hollered for every footmen.

While that was being accomplished, he pointed to the scullery maid. "You, go to the stables and tell them to mount some horses."

"Nobody's there," Spec informed him, handing a pair of pistols to Charles.

They were leaving the foyer when they stopped by the cook's arrival. Mrs. Halstead scurried in and dipped a small curtsy. "Your lordship, if you please—Miss Montgomery came to ask me if I'd seen Arianna. I told her I hadn't. She said they'd been in the gardens. Next thing I knowed, I looked through the window and I seen Miss Montgomery walking towards the fairies pond. Flynn and James and Rupert trailing her. She...she had a pistol, your lordship."

All of Canon Ashby's servants turned out, congregating in the foyer or the main stairwell.

"We believe Sir David's kidnapped my daughter and Miss Montgomery," Charles announced. "They must be found before he hurts them. He's dangerous."

"Lawks!" said Mrs. Halstead.

Not missing a beat, his brother ordered the female servants to form a search party. "Make for the pond. Report back to Bertram if you find anything."

The parcel of fretting maids filed outside, calling for Arianna and Miss Montgomery as they went.

"Where could they be?" Charles demanded. "Where are you going, Mama?"

Lady Northampton's pace didn't slow as she hurried out the front door and raced down the gravel drive. "I'm off to find my granddaughter!"

He and Will exchanged exasperated looks before he shouted, "Mama! Mama, wait. Let Will harness the team and take the coach."

"Very well," she snapped. "But be quick about it!"

Will's blond brows spiked toward his receding hairline, but he stopped to deliver one last instruction. "Bertram, have the footmen conduct a thorough search of the house then send them out in pairs to the north, south, east, and west property lines. Search in ninety degree sweeps to the next compass point. Signal once they find something."

The two brothers walked outside Canon Ashby, retrieving horses from the stable.

"Do you think Sir David has Arianna and Winsome?"

"Why else would Winsome arm herself?" Charles beckoned Lightning. "Did he steal my daughter in the hopes of luring Winsome into his reach?"

The earl made an irritated gesture. "How the hell did he escape?"

"They say he over-powered a guard when the poor bloke un-did Sir David's shackles."

"How's the guard?"

"Fine now, I suppose." Swinging his saddle over Lightning's back, Charles took the time to give the horse a quick pat. "Sorry, old man. You'll have a proper rub down later. With oats." He fastened the buckles while he addressed his brother. "Spec and I will ride out to the fairies pond. Meet us at Landry's once you get the team harnessed."

"Right," Northampton said. "Good luck."

"You too. And Will?"

"Yes?"

"If you see the bastard, take him down." Without waiting to see his brother's reaction, Charles reined Lightning around and with Spec and Buttercup trotted toward the pond, pulling up to ask the female servants if they saw anything.

"There's a set of footprints." One of the maids called out.

"Where are they heading?" Spec hollered.

She pointed eastward—Landry's property.

"Damnation." He turned Lightning in that direction, spurring him toward greater speed.

"Gamekeeper's hut?" Spec guessed, patting his saddle holster.

He might have responded, Charles wasn't certain. They cantered across Northampton's land. Throughout the ride, he pictured the many ways in which he would kill Sir David. If he harmed one yellow hair on Arianna's head or touched Winsome…

They approached a rise in the land. From its height he spied movement on the horizon and swerved toward it. Lightning reared as he yanked the reins like a raw recruit, but the sight of the footman carrying his daughter jarred him. After getting his mount under control, he waved Spec on while he dismounted for Arianna.

She was crying. Sobbing, more like. Taking great, big shuddering breaths. He'd kill Sir David for that alone.

He reached for his daughter as James handed her over, patting her back. The footman's breathing was labored and Charles surmised he must have run a great distance.

"There, there. You're safe." Without planning it, both men chose the same phrase to quiet the girl.

Arianna wailed, "Papa! Oh, Papa, Papa."

"Are you hurt?" Charles tamped down the emotions which threatened to swamp him.

Too riled to answer, she shook her head. Her thin arms around his neck threatened to choke him.

Rocking her, he repeated the question to James. "Was she hurt?"

"Scared, but not hurt. She fell down." He pointed to Arianna's dirty knees.

"Where's Winsome?"

James pointed in the direction Spec rode. Buttercup kicked up a cloud of dust as it raced toward a small group of people. Charles pivoted, standing square to the scene, wishing he were closer. Squinting to see more clearly, he watched as a man in shirtsleeves knelt in the field. He was hunched over a pool—what was it? That wasn't the color of water.

"Oh, God."

That 'pool' was Winsome's dress. Sir David was straddling her while she lay on her back in a tilled field.

He pressed Arianna's face into his shoulder so she couldn't see what he was seeing. At the same time, a shout erupted from him. It was a wounded cry, followed by the report of a short carbine firing.

Arianna started at the sounds and tightened her hold on his neck.

The man in shirt sleeves—Sir David—slumped then toppled forward, his body flopping on the ground. The whole scene had a sense of unreality.

Charles strode in that direction. He hadn't taken more than two steps before he realized he couldn't bring Arianna to that place.

"Take her, James. Sweetheart, go with him." He tried to pry his daughter's arms off him.

She resisted mightily.

"James will take you to Uncle Will."

Arianna shook her head. "NO! Don't leave me, Papa!"

"I have to check on Winsome, Miss Monty. You may stay here with James. He will keep you safe."

"No, no," she sobbed.

"Arianna, you are my daughter. You hear me? A soldier's daughter." He injected as much steel in his voice as he could. "You must be brave, darling. I won't leave your sight, but I must see to Miss Monty. I must."

She wiped her nose on his jacket, hiccupped, and said, "Yes, Papa. I...can...be brave."

He kissed the tip of her nose. "Good girl."

James lifted her into his arms again. He guided her head to his shoulder and she clung to his neck. "I got you. James has you."

Giving the footman a grateful look, Charles mounted Lightning and spurred him to cover the distance. By the time he reached the group, Sir David's twitching had lessened.

"He's in the death throes now," Spec said quietly, explaining the phenomena to Rupert, who watched in horror.

Sir David clutched his neck, his eyes wide with panic as blood poured from his wound. He made as if to speak, but emitted a gurgling sound instead. His eyes dulled, the hand dropped to his chest.

Dismounting close by, Charles made his way to Winsome, who lay in the dirt, still and bloody. "Was she shot? What happened?"

Rupert, kneeling beside Winsome, explained, "No, that's his blood, not hers. He backhanded her."

"Devil take him." Charles crouched over her, lightly patting her cheeks. "Winsome?"

She didn't stir.

He leaned down, listening for sounds of her breathing. Charles sat back on his haunches, a broad smile of relief breaking over his face.

"She's alive, thank God."

Jeb jogged up to the group, carrying the short carbine.

"Nice shooting, boss." Rupert's voice held tones of wonder.

"Damned bloody mess, if you ask me," Spec chimed.

Charles flung up his hand. "It's done. That's all that matters. Line up and form a wall. I don't want Arianna to see this. Flynn, fetch water for Miss Montgomery."

Frowning at her pallor, Charles brushed the dirt from Winsome's cheek then tucked a loose strand behind her ear. As his fingertips passed over a swollen knot, he peered more closely. The tip of her ear bled and worse of all, she hadn't flinched when he skimmed the bruised lump.

"She's concussed," he said. "See here?"

Rupert leaned over and whistled. "Vicious brute," he muttered, throwing a dark glance at Sir David.

"Who shot him in the neck?"

"Jeb." Rupert pointed to the nearby groom.

Flynn rejoined them, sloshing water from a pail.

"And the shoulder?" He thanked the Scotsman.

"Miss Monty."

"Good Lord." Charles dipped his handkerchief into the bucket and dabbed Winsome's face.

She didn't stir.

He submerged the handkerchief then wrung it out and placed it over her forehead.

"We need to bring Miss Montgomery home," Spec suggested. "She'll have the devil of a headache when she comes to, mark my words."

"Yes. The earl should be following in his coach. Let's wait 'til he arrives."

Jeb stared at the lifeless baronet, chewing the insides of his cheek. "What do you want done with him?"

"To hell with him." Spec spat on the ground, not bothering to hide his contempt for Sir David. Then he turned away, re-mounting his horse. "I'll return to Canon Ashby, give Buttercup a well-deserved rub down then select another mount to bring the doctor from Culworth for Miss Montgomery."

"Good. You do that."

Spec mounted Buttercup, but stayed as Jeb argued, "We can't leave a dead body out in the field."

"No." Charles sighed, anxious for his brother to show up with the carriage. "Jeb, you and Flynn find Landry. Tell him what happened. Hell and blast." He stared at Spec. "Landry's already arranging Lady Broomstead's funeral."

Spec shrugged, not overly concerned with Mr. Landry being inconvenienced. "Serves the blighter right for inviting them to the neighborhood. Just as easy to arrange two funerals as it is one."

A humorless laugh escaped him, but he heard the jangle of harnesses and spied the carriage approaching. "Tell Landry to collect the body. We're heading home."

Jeb hesitated, staring at the man he'd killed.

Leaning on his saddle horn, Spec told the groom, "Killed his wife with his own bare hands. You put him down, Jeb, like a rapid dog. You deserve an ale, by God."

"Rabid dog," Charles corrected. "And he's right. Rupert, bring me the carriage blankets. Quickly, lad."

Charles flung out his hand to stop his mother rushing toward them. "Stay back!"

"Oh, my stars!" Her hand covered her mouth.

"Good God!" Will checked his stride.

"She's not been shot. Arianna's fine. Go fetch her from James."

Rupert trotted back, carrying blankets.

He spread one out over Winsome then lifted her. "Cover Broomstead."

"She's so pale," Rupert said, laying the blanket atop the baronet's corpse.

He wished she'd wake up, the sooner the better. Over his shoulder, he told his brother to bring Arianna. "It's time we all went home."

Charles sat in the carriage with his betrothal nestled against him, the blanket tucked about her. In the silence before his family joined them, he whispered, "Come back to me, Winsome."

Chapter 19

Winnie remembered bits and pieces of the ride back to Canon Ashby. Lady Northampton's tucking the quilt beneath her chin, Arianna asking if Miss Mama would be all right, the staff swarming them upon arrival. Through it all she remained in Charles' arms.

When her lashes lifted, his was the first face she saw. His brown eyes glowed with a tender light, but his smile was uncertain.

"Behold," he said in that low, rich voice. "Sleeping Beauty awakes."

"How's Miss Mama?" Arianna asked, pulling back the quilt to take a peek.

"She's fine, Arianna, but we must be very, very quiet. Whispers only, please."

"Arianna." Winnie struggled to free her hand then stroked the girl's tear-stained cheek.

"Yes, Miss Mama. I'm here," Arianna whispered.

"You were so brave. I'm so proud of you, Arianna."

Very solemnly, she nodded and reminded her governess, "I'm a soldier's daughter."

Winnie's smile was faint until it vanished when she touched her temple. "Ow."

Charles flinched in sympathy.

"Sir David? He...he...I shot him, didn't I?"

"That's what I heard."

"Where is he?"

He hushed her. "Don't worry about him. We'll talk about it later."

"I have a monstrous headache."

Charles carried her to her room then quietly explained to a maid she would have to act as Winsome's abigail. She agreed until she saw Winnie's dress. The maid darted from the room, shrieking.

"My head," she groaned.

"Hang the chit," Charles growled, only remembering to lower his voice at the last minute. He propped Winnie against a bedpost and removed her clothes. He folded her dress inside the quilt so she wouldn't have to see the blood splatters.

Silent tears spilled down her cheeks. "My head hurts so…"

"I'll be right back." Charles sat her on the bed then slipped out the chambers and returned within a few moments with his mother.

"Oh, Charles! What were you thinking?" The countess exclaimed. "Oh, I apologize, my dear."

In a whisper, she turned toward her son and instructed him to have the housekeeper send up another maid with tea and powders. "Come, Winnie. Let's get you into bed."

Within moments, the countess had dressed her in her favorite flannel night rail, plumped the pillows behind her back and opened the window to allow the afternoon breeze into the room. She persuaded Winnie to drink a cup of warm tea and a tisane prepared by the cook, Mrs. Halstead then shooed her son from the chambers.

"It's not proper," she hissed, closing the door on Charles' protestations.

Drowsy, Winnie slept.

When she woke it was early evening. She gingerly touched the raw spot above her ear. It was still swollen and sore, but overall, the throbbing had lessened. Moaning, she levered herself against her pillows, just as a maid entered, carrying a supper tray.

"Good evening, Miss Montgomery. Good to see you're awake."

"I'm hungry, Matilda. Thank you."

She set down the tray. "After you've eaten, shall I arrange for a bath?"

"Oh, please. And could I have another one of cook's tisane? That greatly helped my head."

"And probably aided your sleep." She chuckled. "Mrs. Halstead puts scotch whisky in her tisane."

Winnie made a weak smile, finding it ironic she'd come full circle with Charles. Next thing she knew, he'd waltz through that door with his oh-so-broad shoulders and accuse her of tippling.

She ate a good, restorative meal of beef broth and bread then Matilda helped her bathe. It took an age to complete the small task, but Winnie found her aches were easier to deal with at a slower pace. Thankfully, Matilda was a patient woman. Once regowned, the maid then pinned Winnie's hair away from the injured area then dabbed salve on it.

Exhausted, Winnie assured the maid she wouldn't need a lit candle and quickly fell asleep.

Her dreams took her to the fairies pond. In the shade of the hawthorn tree, everything took on a sinister quality. She saw Sir David in profile. He was laughing, but she heard no sound. Winnie felt anger mixed with fear, but the fear wasn't for herself. It was for others.

She was pulled inside a warm cocoon, away from Sir David's chilling presence. It was cozy in this spot, her whole body surrounded by heat and a masculine scent. A pair of strong hands skimmed over her, banishing the anxieties as they roamed.

"Winsome."

Called from the deepest layers of sleep, she heard Charles' rich voice next to her ear. She lifted her eyelashes and gave him a smile. He'd crept into bed, his warm, naked body pressed against hers. What a lovely way to awaken.

"Mm," she said as he nuzzled her neck. Her eyelashes fluttered shut. "Thank you, Charles."

A muffled chuckle. "For what? I didn't do anything."

Heaving a deep sigh of contentment, Winnie said, "You came back for me."

His hand ran along her throat then pressed soft kisses there. Studying her, he asked, "Are you in pain? Am I hurting you?"

"Oh, no." Her fingertips drifted along his shoulders. She lifted her face for his kiss.

He obliged on the instant.

They kissed deeply, slowly, assuring one another. Charles treated her with such care and tenderness that Winnie's eyes filled with unshed tears.

"Don't cry, my love." Charles soothed, cupping her shoulder then running his hand over her ribcage. "All is well."

"Arianna's safe, isn't she? I didn't just imagine that, did I?"

"Yes, I stayed with her until she fell asleep."

"What's become of Sir David?"

"Jeb shot him."

"Fatally?"

"Yes."

Oddly, she had no reaction to this news. She ran her hands over his chest, playing before she remarked, "Stanhope will sit empty, I suppose. I don't know who Sir David's heir is."

"Mm."

"Perhaps that's all to the good? Break the chain, as it were."

"We have our own problems to worry about," he said.

"We do? What problems?"

He kissed her again, long and hard then lay on his back. Tucking her into his side, he said, "We're not going to marry by special license. I can't face the thought of leaving you even for a few days and you're in no condition to travel to London, which means we'll have the banns read."

"Which means it'll be three weeks until we're wed."

He groaned. "Three weeks."

Her palm smoothed over his torso, trailing to his hip and moving tantalizingly close to his manhood. "If you expect us to remain chaste these next few weeks, why did you place your naked self in my bed?"

"First of all, I always sleep in the nude. Second, I had to make sure you were all right. You did the same with me, remember?"

Winnie giggled before agreeing, "Of course."

"Thirdly, between you and Arianna, I had the scare of my life today. I need some comfort."

His sheepish look may or may not have been genuine. Smiling, she kissed his chin and murmured, "My poor darling."

Smirking, he spread the flannel neckline to gaze at her breasts. Using the back of his knuckle, he grazed her nipple, watching it harden and peak. "God, I love you."

"Make love to me, Charles."

His head tilted as if he were considering the matter. The lines beside his mouth pulled down as he regretfully informed her, "I don't think that would be wise, given your headache…"

"If you're gentle…"

"I'd be gentle," he promptly promised.

"And go slowly."

"I will. Oh, God, yes, I will."

Smiling the tiniest bit, Winnie couldn't help but relish the feminine power she held over him. It worked both ways. She removed her nightgown, cautioning him in a whisper, "We must be quiet so no one discovers."

His hand reached to her center. As his long fingers trailed the intimate passages, he stared at her. The solemnity of his expression surprised her. "Are you certain, Winsome?"

"Yes, just go slowly."

He rubbed the sensitive area with his fingers then one by one, his fingers sank into those depths. His thumb spread her dew until she arched in response and bucked against his hand.

When she felt she could endure no more, his mouth latched onto her nipple. He threw it into his mouth and suckled. Shoots of pleasures spiked from her breast and coursed through her body. Even her scalp tingled from his ministrations. His hand continued to work in her as his tongue traveled to her other breast.

She hissed in pleasure, tamping down the impulse to moan aloud.

Moving over her in gradual degrees, Charles' hands and mouth touched every inch of her skin. His calloused palms arranged her limbs in various poses as he explored her body. Her temperature climbed. Delicious ripples moved through her body, passing like sunlight through water. Charles kept her on a knife's edge, stoking the passions then allowing them to subside then rebuilding them again.

It was all she could do to keep quiet. And he knew it. That mocking gleam in his eyes taunted her with her own admonition and more than anything else, Winnie wished for the relief of shouting her joy.

With her knees bent and thighs parted wide, his dark head lowered above the plane of her stomach. As he drank from her core, tonguing her in maddening, slow movements, she bit her lip to keep from screaming. Slowly and gently, he was driving her to the brink of madness. Never again would she extend such a challenge to Charles.

"Charles," she panted, dazed.

He didn't stop.

She thrust her hands into his hair, feeling those internal muscles throb until she broke rhythm. "Charles!"

She bucked, but he returned, his tongue delving deeper into her until the vortex of emotions swept her up and carried her over the edge. Waves of sensation broke as the last quiver left her body.

Charles received the gift, gazing at her with a look of utter tenderness.

Spent, the scent of her arousal filled the room along with the muted sound of her ragged breathing. She blink, amazed at the transformation he unleashed within her. "Please, Charles, oh please."

The simple words had a profound effect on him. Gone was the teasing light in those brown eyes. Charles rose above her, bracing himself on his forearms then slid into her in a smooth, long thrust. Fully sheathed, he stayed put, the strain of doing so causing him to tremble.

Her legs wrapped around his waist, bringing him closer as she held him fiercely.

He established the pace, gliding in and pulling out then plunging in again.

Winnie shuddered from happiness, closing her eyes and savoring each stroke, matching his rhythm. She pressed her lips against his collarbone to smother her cries of passion. Together they traveled, back and forth, making their way up the mountaintop, not so much by inches, but by leaps and bounds.

At the pinnacle, they gazed upon a new world. Staring into his warm eyes, she whispered his name.

They hurtled off the mountaintop, tumbling to earth like a pair of fallen angels.

"Winsome," he exhaled.

It felt like a benediction.

Epilogue

Kedington, County Suffolk, Eastern England
March, 1812

"Hand me my grandson," commanded the countess, her arms reaching to take the babe from Winnie. Her mother-in-law cradled the newborn in the crook of her arm, sitting on the long blue sofa in the drawing room. "Oh, what a handful he is! So chubby! Such a precious baby boy!"

Standing on tiptoe, Arianna leaned against the arm of the sofa. She rolled her eyes, not so enamored by her little brother's charms. She pointed out to her dear grandmamma, "He's poopy and cries a lot."

Lady Northampton looked up from blowing kisses to Baby Nicholas. "Is he colicky, dear? You didn't mention that in your letters, Winnie."

"No, no. He's fine," Winnie cast an affectionate look upon her daughter. "Arianna's heart was set on having a little sister and she still hasn't forgiven Nicholas for being a boy."

"Juju refuses to dress him in clothes to match Arianna's, which doesn't help," Charles drawled, handing his brother a glass of brandy. He then crossed the Axminister rug and stood beside Winnie's chair. He placed his warm hand on her shoulder.

Smiling up at her handsome husband, she patted the back of his hand.

After taking a sip, the earl voiced his agreement with his niece. "Little brothers are, indeed, tedious."

"Well, not all the time." The concession was wrung from Arianna. "Sometimes he smiles at me and Mama says Nicholas'll be better when he grows some."

"Don't you believe it, poppet." The earl tapped the tip of Arianna's nose.

Her eyes shining, she hopped in enthusiasm at her new idea. "Will you play spillikens with me, Uncle Will?"

"The fondest wish of my heart," the earl said somberly. "Will you excuse us, please?"

Taking her uncle's hand, Arianna said, "I asked Mrs. Huggins to prepare strawberry tarts—our favorite. Well, they're my favorite, but you enjoy strawberry tarts, too, don't you? You do." She chuckled at his look of dismay and joined him in tossing out casual goodbyes to the room at large. As the little girl led the earl away, Winnie smiled at the conversation. "Have you met our cook, Mrs. Huggins? Her husband works here, too. And the Dobsons? Oh, Uncle! I found a bird's nest with two blue eggs. Blue! Did you know…"

Lady Northampton shook her head. "It's so quiet at Canon Ashby without Arianna! Will has missed her terribly."

"Only Will?" Charles teased. "Mama, we visited Canon Ashby at Michaelmas. Surely you enjoyed a few weeks of quiet?"

"Not at all, Charles." The countess batted away the ludicrous suggestion. "We were most anxious to see the baby."

"Yes, I believe your anticipation rivaled my wife's."

"Charles, stop funning." Winnie *tsked* then addressed the countess again. "We're happy to have you both visit any time, please feel welcome to stay as long as you like."

"Thank you, my dears."

The baby started to root, searching for his next meal. The countess chuckled. "Do you have a wet nurse? I fear Baby Nicholas is hungry."

"We don't have a wet nurse. Winnie feeds him herself." He took the baby from his mother and lightly bounced Nicholas in his arms.

"Is that right? Modern notions," she said thoughtfully, rising from the sofa and tucking a tiny blanket around her grandson. "It appears to be working, so I won't quibble with success."

"Thank you, Mama," Winnie accepted the compliment.

The countess gave her a knowing look. "In fact, everyone appears to be very happy. Didn't I tell you, Charles, that my hiring Winnie was a stroke of genius?"

"Yes, Mama," Charles grinned. He assisted Winnie from her chair.

"While you tend to Nicholas, I believe I'll have a lie-in before dinner."

"With any luck, Nick will nap, too," Winnie said.

"Allow us to escort you to your rooms, Mama."

Charles nodded for his mother to precede them and they chatted as they strolled upstairs. After leaving his mama, they went to their suite. They entered their private rooms, which were painted cream and gold. Upon their marriage, Winnie placed the Gainsborough painting above the mantel in their private sitting room. She draped the bed and windows in persimmon-colored silk, matching her grandmother's gown in the landscape. Their suite was one of her favorite spots on the estate and she thought Charles enjoyed it just as well.

They'd established a routine where, no matter how busy they were throughout the day, they ended the evening together in the suite. After Charles read a bedtime story to Arianna, he'd join Winnie on the sofa where they'd cuddle before the fire. They'd talk, laugh, sip tea, or toast crumpets. When they married, Winnie's heart was so full, she thought it'd burst. As she watched her husband place Baby Nicholas in his wooden cradle, that same organ expanded, as it had every day since marrying Charles.

"Hush, little man. Patience," he counseled his son. Charles came to her and began unlacing her dress for the feeding.

"You're more proficient than my abigail," she said drily.

"It's a matter of being properly motivated. Military hero and all that." He kissed her bare shoulder.

"Mm." She stretched her neck, giving him greater access.

They might have lost themselves for a few heavenly moments if not for the baby's cries.

"Sorry, fella," Charles chuckled, removing Winnie's gown entirely.

She stepped out of it, protesting, "I only needed the bodice lowered; no need to remove the gown entirely."

"Yes, there is, my love. Feed Nicholas then have a rest with me."

He gave her a wicked smile, which she returned in full measure.

Nicholas squalled.

Charles turned his head, murmuring, "Patience."

Clad only in her chemise, Winnie climbed upon the bed and stacked the pillows behind her for better support.

"He's only a baby, dear. What could Nicholas possibly know about patience?"

He waggled his brows. "I was talking to myself, not my son."

Charles brought her the babe, helping to position him then watching as Nicholas nursed. Chuckling, his finger stroked his son's cheek while Nicholas suckled. "He's going to be a lively fellow, isn't he, Mrs. Dryden?"

"Oh, yes." She beamed at him. "He'll be as handsome and as kind as his papa."

"There was a time you didn't think me kind," he teased. "You thought me a flirtatious, drunken gambler."

"You wish to hear me take back those words?" She sent him an arch smile.

"I'm waiting." He lifted his hands.

"But you *are* a flirtatious, drunken gambler."

"How can you say that?"

"You flirt with me all the time, Charles. Admit it."

"Only you."

Winnie's head bounced from side to side, as though that rebuttal proved her point.

"I believe the poets describe the experience as inebriated on love." She moved Nicholas to her other breast.

"Redefining sobriety to gain the upper hand, eh? Very well. Guilty as charge." He *tsked*. "But a gambler? You're out there, my love. Spec and I only ever gamble for pennies, not pounds."

"Ah, but you took a gamble when you married a baronet's daughter."

"Not really." He gathered Nicholas, burped him then resettled him in the cradle. "I was sure you loved me."

"You were not!"

He chuckled then admitted, "No, I wasn't."

She eyed him with mock severity before casually stating, "You know, Charles, today Nicholas is seven weeks old."

He stilled.

The number held particular importance.

"The doctor advised eight weeks."

"Seven or eight weeks," Winnie corrected. "Seven if the husband refrains from teasing his wife."

"I won't tease you ever again," he promptly lied.

Peeking beneath her lashes, she said, "Well, perhaps you may tease me just a bit."

With more speed than grace, Charles removed his jacket, neck cloth, and shirt.

"Oh, my." Winnie caught her breath. "I do love those shoulders so."

Chuckling, he tore off his boots, shucked his britches, and leapt on the bed.

Gurgling with laughter, Winnie lifted her chemise over her head, casting it aside. She stretched her arms above her head, feeling deliciously wanton wearing only a grin and fragrance.

"I'm a lucky man." Her husband pounced and she squealed in delight. He kissed her with long, drugging kisses, his hands cupping her hips and passing over her buttocks.

As he touched her, those lovely sensations traveled through Winnie. Hungry for him, too, her hands roamed his beautiful, muscular body as the heat grew. Flesh pressed against flesh, their joining created a new world, which encompassed only the two of them. Their passion remained fiery, but Winnie sensed a difference in their lovemaking. The intensity remained, but there was no great urgency goading her to climax. Charles seemed equally content to focus on the journey, rather than the finish. His mouth and hands worked their usual magic, caressing her, melding their bodies into one. There was satisfaction and enjoyment without that tiny bit of anxiety, which accompanied their previous couplings.

"Something's different, Charles—what is it?"

"Every time feels different with you, Winsome." He reached between them and used his thumb to circle the hood of her sex.

"Yes, but—" She gasped, her eyes opening wide. "You're so big, Charles!"

Gritting his teeth, he pulled back slightly. "I'm not hurting you, am I?"

"No," she quickly denied, gathering him closer.

"God, Winsome."

"I know."

In a startling move, he flipped them over so that she was on top.

He thrust deeper into her, so deep she thought he'd touched virgin territory.

"Oh!"

Charles spanned her waist, lifting and lowering her along his cock until she moaned. She found her rhythm and rode him. He groaned. His grip tightened and his face tensed. She moved against him, hard, then launched off the peak as his hot seed poured into her.

Damp with sweat, she collapsed onto his chest as he hissed in completion. They remained joined. She had neither the desire nor the energy to climb off her husband.

"Winsome." He touched her hair. "I love you."

"And I love you."

They grew silent and still, soaking up the nuances of all the scattered sensations.

Finally, she whispered, "I know what the difference is."

He caught some loose strands of her hair, rubbing them between his thumb and forefinger. "Different good or different bad?"

She playfully smacked his shoulder at the silly question, but to make certain there could be no murkiness on this point, she clarified, "Good."

"What is it?"

"Because I've accepted my lot in life." She shrugged as she explained, "To be deeply loved by you and the children."

His warm chuckle made her smile, as did the strength she'd always find in his embrace.

"Then you are a lucky woman. Now go to sleep, dear wife."

"Yes." The corner of her mouth quirked as Charles planted a quick kiss there. "How lucky we are."

The End

Made in the USA
Lexington, KY
22 August 2017